Copyright© 2023 Sam Crescent

ISBN: 978-0-3695-0814-0

Cover Artist: Jay Aheer

Editor: Karyn White

ALL RIGHTS RESERVED

BROKEN PROMISE

BROKEN PROMISE

The Denton Family Legacy, 1

Sam Crescent

Copyright © 2016

Chapter One

"Are you a fucking Denton, or are you a pussy? We don't have pussies in the family, Landon," Jacob Denton said to his youngest brother. The Denton name was a well respected name, and they were known for not taking shit from anybody. Their legacy had begun many years ago with his great-grandfather, or maybe even before that. They were all respected, feared, and admired wherever they went. Jacob liked the attention. He needed it.

They were not actors or models or singers. He along, with his five brothers and one sister, were part of an empire that spanned over several cities, and they had their noses in a lot of other people's businesses. Some would say they were the bad guys, and mothers should really lock their houses when they heard a Denton was coming.

"I'm not a fucking pussy. I'm a monster," Landon said, screaming out. Anyone looking at his youngest brother would believe he was a hell of a lot older than his sixteen years. Almost every single family would be horrified if they found out that their teenage son competed in an underground fight with someone who was a hell of a lot older. This was the Denton way. Their father had done this, and so had Jacob, Abel, Oliver, Gideon, and Damian. It was now Landon's turn to not only prove himself to the family, but also get the same reputation for the world to see. The only person in the family who wouldn't be in this ring would be Tamsin.

"Don't fuck with a Denton," people said. They were a crime family, a deadly mix that ruled with an iron fist. Jacob trusted his brothers, no one else. They had friends, but none they could trust as much as each other. Their father made sure there was no rivalry between them. They were all equal to him, and he never showed favoritism.

"That's right, son, you're the animal here," Maddox Denton, their father and head of the Denton Legacy said. "You show them that no Denton will be beat."

Landon growled out, and Jacob stood back, standing by his brothers as he watched him go back to fight his opponent. Abel had his hand ready on his gun to start fighting if shit hit the fan. They had all been in this place, and neither one of them had lost, but none of them looked as bad as Landon. For the first time in his thirty-five years, Jacob felt uneasy. No Denton had ever lost at a fight. Landon was just like them, but he was letting the fucker land punches when it wasn't necessary.

"He's doing it on purpose," Damian said. "He's feeding off the anger, besides, he wants to make Mom and Dad proud."

Jacob looked toward the luxurious changing rooms to see his mother, Charlotte, with her arms wrapped around herself. Bruce, her bodyguard, stood beside her, keeping a watch for any potential threat. If their father could have, he'd have locked their mother in a tower so only her family saw her, he was that protective. Jacob knew it was hard for his father to allow another male to be close to her as that was another thing about their legacy, and what unnerved their enemies at times. Most families with dealings like theirs were known to be unstable, users, and passing whores around like they were going out of fashion. The Dentons, all of them, didn't do that. Once they found that one woman there was no one else for them. Jacob had witnessed the love between his parents, and it rivaled those of the greatest love stories on the big screen.

"Block him, Landon," Maddox said, yelling advice.

This was why his mother should never come to the fights, but she always did when it involved her kids. Landon had three blows landed to his face, and it looked like he was about to go down, but he paused. Jacob watched as Landon attacked, slamming his fist against his opponent's face, working him over. The monster had been unleashed, and even Jacob was taken aback by the sheer violence in his baby brother.

Blow after blow after blow. There was no stopping the violence. The rage crossed Landon's face, and when the whistle blew and he showed no sign of stopping Maddox ran into the ring and grabbed his son.

"Landon, enough!" Maddox held his son, and Jacob took over so their father could get Landon. When that didn't work, their mother was suddenly in front of them, and she clapped her hands in front of Landon's face, bringing their brother back.

Reality returned to Landon, and he nodded. "I'm good. I'm good."

Stepping out of the ring, Jacob joined his brothers

as his father showed off his latest son who had won the fight.

"He needs a woman and fast," Abel said.

"Only *his* woman can handle that fucking monster. Look at Mom with Dad. She's the only one who can talk sense into him," Gideon said.

Jacob couldn't argue with his brothers. Landon had an easy, quick temper that had caused their parents a headache a time or two. He seemed to like to take a beating, and once that was done, he'd smack the shit out of them. Since Landon had made it to high school, he'd gotten into over a dozen fights, and put three guys in the hospital. Maddox had to pay a shitload of money out in compensation, to keep Landon from going to prison or juvy. Only a woman would be able to tame the monster inside Landon, but it was something none of them could get him. They could supply him with all the pussy the city could buy, but if his woman wasn't a whore, or fucking easy, then they couldn't do it.

"Thank you all for coming. I expect big things from Landon, and you be sure to talk about the latest addition to the Denton Empire," Maddox said. The crowd went wild, and then they were moving toward their exclusive rooms.

"What the hell was that?" Charlotte asked.

Landon sat down on a bench, unwrapping his hands as he spat blood onto the ground. "Fucker had it coming."

"Watch your language," Maddox said.

Charlotte took the first aid kit from the doctor and got to work fixing up her son. Even though they paid a lot for the best doctor it was always Charlotte who fixed them up. Their mother was once a trained nurse, and even though she no longer worked in a hospital, she kept her license and training up to date.

"That fucker as you call him, Landon, is a Moore boy."

"Moore?" Jacob asked. "Fuck, I should have known." The Moores were a mixed bag of good and bad. They were a family who dealt with fights, but they also created a lot of enemies.

"His family is known for their skill at fighting. He's an expert, and he offered to go into the ring with you when no one else would. You fought dirty tonight, and not like a Denton."

Once their mother got started on a tirade, it was best to see it through. At fifty-three years old, she was still a beautiful woman, but then she hadn't allowed their lifestyle to lure her down the spiral of drugs and booze. She didn't go out spending thousands of dollars on shit she didn't need. Charlotte still cooked for her family, and made sure they didn't allow the power they all had to go to their heads. She kept them stable, which also unnerved their enemies. They were unpredictable and deadly without the need for narcotics.

"You may think you won that fight, and you made us proud. You may have even made your father proud, and those people out there all happy with the latest addition to the family empire. As far as I'm concerned, tonight you put shame on the Denton name. When a man is down, you walk the fuck away, do you hear me?" She grabbed Landon's face and forced him to look at her. "You're better than an animal, Landon. Do not ever let me be ashamed of you again, do you understand?"

"Yes, Mom," Landon said. There was no attitude or tone to his voice. He'd been stripped down.

Maddox squeezed her shoulder. Over the years Jacob had noticed those little touches. His father couldn't go any length of time without touching his woman. It was like he couldn't help but reach out to her.

His parents' love had kept them all safe, and if anything was to ever happen to his mother, Maddox would go crazy. The Dentons lived with a legacy to love one woman, and in their history, it showed they went off the rails if something was to happen to that woman.

Jacob didn't know how he was ever to find the one woman meant for him, but his father, and uncles all told him that the moment he saw her, he'd just know. There would be an impulse, a need to have her, to take her, to care for her. There would be no stopping in his need to claim his woman.

In the last thirty-five years he'd experienced lust and even believed he was in love, but he'd never been consumed by the way his father and uncles were with their women.

There were times like now when the world was moving around him so fast that he wondered what it would be like, to experience such need for another. The women he'd fucked had held his attention for as long as it took to fuck them and forget about them. He loved sex. He loved fucking, and he loved women that were easy. It was the one area where he was the cliché crime boss. He had a little black book full of sluts who'd take his cock without any question. There had even been women he called who were in the middle of fucking one man, and they'd climbed right off to come to him.

He was an asshole, arrogant, and he didn't give a shit what people thought about him.

"Good. I only want to hear the best of my sons." Charlotte stared at each of them. Tamsin, their baby sister, was the only one missing, and she was at home with the babysitter.

"Come on, honey, let's leave the boys to their fun." Their father took hold of their mother, leading her away.

"Well, Landon, do you think you're ready to fuck?" Damian asked.

The celebrations were about to begin.

****

"What the hell was that?" Louisa, Lou to her friends, Moore asked her brother.

Riley had asked her to come to the fight, and she hadn't expected her twin brother to be fighting a Denton. Her family didn't have much to do with the famous crime family, but they had a lot to do with fighting. At twenty-five years old, Riley shouldn't have been fighting a sixteen year old. "No one would fight him."

"He's a sixteen year old boy. He's not even out of high school. If I'd known this, I'd have put a stop to it." She pressed a cloth to his bleeding mouth and winced as she looked at the mess of her twin. He was older than she was by one minute, but he always behaved like she was the baby.

"Mom and Dad wanted this. It was a show of strength."

"It was a show of stupidity. Sixteen, Riley, fucking sixteen. What did you hope to achieve?"

"Nothing like my sister who has let the family down by not marrying well," Riley said, spitting more blood out.

Lou growled. "This is my life, and I don't have to marry who they tell me to."

"Mom and Dad are going to pick you out a husband."

"Mom and Dad can go and screw themselves, or their respective mistresses and lovers. I don't give a shit. This is my life, and I'm not ending up like them." Their parents hated each other, but they'd been arranged to be married when they were younger. Lou was determined never to end up like them, and she was going to marry a man she loved, respected, and who was not part of the underground fighting lifestyle.

She stared at her brother's beaten face, and she felt so damn angry.

"No one would fight Landon. This is good for our family." It would be the only good thing. Everything to do with the Moores was tainted.

"That's because Landon is a loose cannon." She'd heard about the youngest brother of the Denton clan, and she wasn't impressed. When thinking about the ultimate empire family, she didn't like them. They were violent thugs.

"Regardless, I'm now known for standing up against one of the worst Dentons since Jacob."

Lou paused. "Seriously? This is what this is about? Some kind of title? A reputation?"

"No one else has it."

"Ugh, I hate men. You don't care about anything but your stupid titles, and names, and ugh." She threw the towel at him and stormed away.

"This is all it has ever been about, Lou."

She turned back to face him to see him holding a towel against his face. This she hated to see. The bruises on her brother's face, the blood, the pain. It was all a mark of violence that her family was a part of. Years ago when she was a little girl, she'd been oblivious to her parents' dislike of each other. She hadn't known about the fighting or their connection to one of the biggest crime families the States had ever seen. The Dentons were vicious, and yet even despite their viciousness, they were all reported to have a sweet side. Rumor had it that only one woman could snag a Denton, and he would go out of his way to make sure she was loved and protected. She figured it was a bunch of bullshit.

Lou never listened to rumors. She hadn't even met a Denton yet. Well, that wasn't entirely true. She'd not seen a Denton in over fifteen years, and that had been Abel, the second in line to the throne.

"What are you going to do when they smash your face in one too many times?" she asked.

Riley didn't say anything, just like she knew he wouldn't. Most of the time she stayed out of the family business, and the only reason she was here tonight was because it beat being at her apartment, worried sick over him. She had been at the gym owned by her parents when she heard that her brother was fighting tonight. To everyone's amusement, she'd been trying to slim down from her size eighteen curves, but it seemed no matter what she did, she couldn't shed the weight.

She'd hoped with exercise she'd be able to eat as much fried chicken and chocolate as she wanted, but that was not the case. Sure, she could work out, and eat, but she would have to work out every single hour of every single day to even lose a pound. She hated food. No, that was an entire pack of lies. *She* loved food, but her body hated it.

Pushing her own thoughts aside, she stared at her brother.

"This is all part of the business."

"I know what it is or isn't, Riley. I'm not asking you to tell me what you're doing isn't wrong. I want to know what you're going to do when this goes too far. That ring is not governed by law. It's got its own set of rules."

Riley reached out, holding her hand. "I'm not going to fight any time soon."

Tears filled her eyes. "People die from fighting."

"I'm a tough old fucker, Lou. Nothing is going to kill me."

She shook her head, reaching out to take his face, gently. "Don't do anything stupid."

"I'm not going to, but I am going to the after party hosted at the Dentons' house. It's why Mom and Dad couldn't be here. They're making sure they are there before anyone can throw them out."

"You mean in case you had won the fight and the baby hadn't?" Lou asked.

Riley sighed. "You just don't get it, but maybe one day you will."

"If you're thinking when my kids are old enough to do this shit, you better think again. I'm not letting my kids do anything like this."

Her brother laughed. "Go and wait in the car. I'll be out in a minute. Don't want to miss an opportunity to rub it into every fucker's face that they were too damn scared to take on the sixteen year old boy."

"You do know how that sounds, right?"

"You didn't even watch the fight. You have no idea what he looks like."

She hadn't been able to watch the fight. The thought of her brother fighting someone so young hadn't appealed to her. She'd stayed in his dressing room, listening to the screaming and yelling. They were all animals. "True."

"Go and wait in the car. I'll be there in a minute."

"Pfft, you can't even walk."

Riley climbed off the table and raised his brow at her. "Got a problem?"

"Fine, I'll go and wait in the car." She turned on her heel and walked out of the back of the changing rooms to where his car was. Climbing into the passenger side, she tapped her legs as she waited. This was what she never wanted to do. From the moment she first realized what her parents did, she'd been fighting to stay away from them.

Many of the argument she had with her parents were because she refused to fall in line and accept her fate. She wasn't going to become another trophy wife, or a connection to another crime family. Her parents didn't like the fact she had a free mind, or that she intended to do what she wanted to do rather than what she had been told.

Pushing her hair out of her face, she pulled it on top of her head so it wouldn't be in the way.

She didn't have to wait long before Riley was in the car. "I figured you'd try to drive my car."

She chuckled. "There's only so far a brother's love will get me, and taking his car for a drive will test that love."

"You got that right."

He fired up the engine, and she sat back, enjoying the ride of the car.

Chapter Two

Jacob grabbed a beer and looked around the large reception room which was filled with people. The fight meant they were in for one hell of a party, and glancing across the room, he saw that Landon was already lapping up the attention. Three women were all hanging around him.

"He's certainly the life and soul of the party," Gideon said.

Turning to his brother, he raised his beer, but didn't take a sip. "He's earned it."

"We knew he was going to earn it."

"Did we?" Jacob asked. "He looked ready to give up."

"Nah, it's Landon's MO. He likes to make people think he's defeated, and then bam, they're fucked. It's beautiful to watch."

Releasing a sigh, Jacob glanced toward the door waiting for Riley Moore to arrive. It was always a sign of respect to allow the opponent to party with them. Riley had put up a good fight, and Jacob actually liked him. He was a good man, and he wasn't searching for the wrong kind of attention either. Jacob hadn't recognized him earlier, as his focus had been on his brother. Riley was one of the few Moores that Jacob could actually stand.

"Landon has a bad reputation." Jacob had heard all about Landon's temper, and he'd seen him do crazier shit than he had in the ring tonight. What he didn't like was his brother's lack of control. They all had a temper, and were all known to be vicious when threatened, but none of them ever lost control like that. Hitting a guy when he was down, it was against the rules, and he was pleased their mother fixed that problem, or at least said shit to make Landon think.

"Yeah, well, none of us are ever going to have a good reputation. Look at Abel, he slit a man's throat in front of the wife, and made her clean the blade. Oliver fucks other men's wives, and if it suits him, he makes them watch while he does. Damian, well, he's just into serious fucking kink, and that speaks for itself."

Jacob laughed. "Okay, so what is your issue? And mine?"

Gideon smiled. "You need to be in control all the time, and me, I'm just perfect."

Rolling his eyes, Jacob looked out at the room full of people kissing each other's asses. He spotted the Moores, who were lapping up the attention that their son had granted them.

"I fucking hate them," he said, nodding toward the Moores. "They're greedy as fuck, and they have gained a lot of enemies."

"It's the human condition."

Rolling his eyes, Jacob made his way out of the room toward the kitchen where he found his mother with his father standing close to her.

"Why did you invite them?" Jacob asked. He was being completely unreasonable, but he didn't give a shit.

"Their son fought Landon," Maddox said.

"So?"

"It's polite to invite the parents along with the failed opponent. I happen to like Riley, and if he ever wanted a job I'd gladly give him one. You'd work well with him, Jacob." Maddox stole a piece of chicken, and Charlotte slapped him on the hand.

"I don't like them here, and they shouldn't be around Tamsin."

"Tamsin is in bed, and we wouldn't let anything hurt our daughter." Charlotte glared at him.

Holding up his hands in surrender, Jacob looked

back out into the chaos. He hated these parties that invited everyone who was big in their illegal field. Jacob recognized several pimps, drug lords, and he noticed lots of guns. His father had never had one of these parties go bad, but they always put him on edge.

The Denton name was a feared one, but that didn't stop them from their fair share of enemies.

"What is it?" Maddox asked.

"We need to talk about the strip clubs."

"What about them?"

Glancing at his mother, Jacob waited for her to leave.

"I'm not going anywhere, Jacob. I'm very much aware of everything your father does. I may not agree with everything he does. I won't hide from it, and I will never be a wife and mother who pretends her sons are good, law-abiding citizens."

"We are good, law-abiding citizens."

Charlotte pointed a knife at him. "You're going to look your mom in the eye, and lie? I seem to recall your broken knuckles two weeks ago, and then let's not forget the fight at one of your gentlemen's clubs. I'm not a fool, Jacob Denton. Do not even think to treat me like one."

"Son, don't even think to cause a problem. I never kept anything from her, and when you find the right woman for you, you'll be the same."

Rolling his eyes, Jacob stormed out of the kitchen into the back garden. He needed some fresh air. Listening to the door open and then close, he groaned.

"What now? Did I upset Mom?" he asked, finding his father stood beside him.

"It's a nice night, and considering you're the oldest, you don't know your mother all that well, do you?"

Jacob shrugged. "I guess not."

"Charlotte has always been a special kind of woman to me. She's the only woman I will ever love."

"I notice you don't say she's the only woman you've ever fucked!"

Maddox slapped him around the back of the head. "Ouch!"

"Respect your mother. No, she's not the only woman I've ever fucked. Before I met her, I screwed around. I was young, and I was an asshole. I didn't believe what my father told me about finding the right woman, just like you. Then I found Charlotte, and she taught me what it really meant to be a man."

Rubbing the back of his head, he glared at his father. Jacob had never been afraid of his father, and he wasn't even afraid now.

"What do you want me to say?" Jacob asked.

"I don't want you to say anything at all. Tell me what is on your mind?"

Jacob sighed. "Nothing. Nothing is on my mind."

"I can't help until you start talking real shit."

Rubbing the back of his head, Jacob stretched up working out his over stressed muscles. He hadn't realized how tense he'd been until that moment. Fuck, he loved his little brother, and he'd never wanted Landon to go through that kind of shit.

"Tamsin doesn't have to fight, does she?" Jacob asked. Even at thirty-five the Denton name still surprised him.

"What the fuck? No. She's a woman. Tamsin doesn't have to prove herself to anyone."

"Are you going to try to marry her off?"

"Even if I wanted to, that's not my decision. Your mother and I, before we had you, when she realized what I was, it took her a long time to adjust."

"Adjust? Mom had me when she was eighteen

years old."

"Nearly nineteen, and you think she wasn't freaking out the whole time?" Maddox asked.

"I met your mother, fell in love, and that love has never once changed or diminished. I'd die for that fucking woman, but I was an asshole, and she didn't have a clue what I was until after Abel was born. Shit got real fucking serious after that."

"What happened?"

"She got scared and took you both away. I didn't see her for six whole weeks. I couldn't find her. It's the first time in my life I ever felt real fear. I wasn't there to protect her."

Jacob hadn't known this. This was one part of his life he didn't actually remember. "What did you do?" he asked.

"I kept on working while trying to find her, but it was never enough. I was always one step behind her. It didn't help that I realized what a total fucker I'd been. I never asked her anything about herself. Just assumed she'd be fucking happy with me. She had a Denton in her life, and I didn't care enough about anything else." Maddox took a deep breath. "After that, I went fucking mental."

Jacob had known about his father's days of being completely crazy. Nearly everyone he met talked about the moment his father showed his true colors of what a Denton could really be.

"How did you get her back?"

"She called me from England. I didn't have a fucking clue that she actually had family over there, and she did." Maddox laughed. "Charlotte called because she'd heard about a certain Denton causing shit over his woman. From that one phone call, I worked my ass off until I finally got her permission to fly out to England."

"Permission? Why didn't you just go?"

"I didn't have a clue where she was. She wouldn't tell me, so I talked to her every single chance I could on the phone. Even being miles away, Charlotte calmed the monster inside of me."

"Monster? You're not a monster."

"Yet I have the respect of thousands the moment I walk into a room. Think about that, Jacob. I'm not a monster to my family, yet to others, I'm the bogeyman they've taught their kids to be afraid of." Maddox took a deep breath, inhaling the warm summer night's air. "I fucking love this time of year. Have you felt it yet?"

"Felt what?"

"The burning need to be with a woman."

"Nope."

"I'm really sorry for you, son," Maddox said.

"Why?"

"You're thirty-five years old. I was twenty when I found your mother."

"And you almost screwed it up."

"You're going to screw it up, son. Just make sure you don't take it too far." Maddox slapped him on the back, and made his way back inside. "I hear the losing party has arrived. Let's go and congratulate him."

"It sounds like we're mocking him more than anything."

"Not at all. Riley Moore as far as I'm concerned is a decent guy, and I had him checked out. He's one hell of a fighter who could have gone all the way if his parents weren't determined to keep him as their prize puppet. I'm about to offer him a job."

Jacob rolled his eyes and entered the house again. The silence that he was enjoying was long gone.

The sound of two women shouting caught and drew his attention. One sounded shrill and like an old cackling witch, but the other, it set his nerves on end and not in a bad way, not at all. Closing his eyes, he took in every single tone of her, which was like sweet music to his ears.

Finally, after what seemed an eternity but was in fact only a few seconds, he opened his eyes, and looked toward the sound.

Everything seemed to slow down as people seemed to move out of his way creating a path. He saw her straight away. Her back was to him. Her long blonde hair fell around her in waves. Even from this far away, he saw how damn curvy she was. Her ass screamed at him to be spanked. Walking toward her, Jacob was determined to have her, no matter what the cost was.

****

"This is the place?" Lou asked.

"Yes. Are you going to make a scene?"

She turned to look over at her beat up twin, and she was already damn angry again, hating her parents. "They're in there?"

"Lou, seriously, I love you, but you don't need to fight this fight."

"I'm not going to fight with anyone, brother. I'm simply not going to take their kind of crap."

"You know they wish you were a boy," Riley said, climbing out of the car.

She followed suit, giving him a big beaming smile. "You do know that I haven't cared that my parents can't stand me. I find it fun."

"Is that why you work at that strip club as a waitress?" Riley asked.

Lou paused, turning back to look at her brother.

"Oh yes, I know about the bar, and I know you slept with a couple of guys they hadn't chosen for you."

She couldn't help but smile. "What you mean is I

slept with people they didn't approve of?" Lou had done everything to try to break the rules. She was tired of living a lie, and so far, her life had been one big fat lie.

"I love you, Lou. You're my sister, my twin. I just don't want you to get hurt. There are people out there who will hurt you just to rub our parents' noses in it."

Shrugging, Lou linked her arm through with his. "Don't care. I love you, too, Riley, even when you're too battered and bruised to realize it."

Riley laughed. "Let's go and impress the masses, and then you've got to disappear. I intend to take a woman home with me tonight."

Wrinkling her nose, she walked into the house, which she'd never been in before. It was huge, like a mansion. She had to wonder if the Dentons' neighbors had any idea who they were living next to. The basement was probably covered in blood and bleach. She shivered and did her best to hide her nerves. This was why she tried to stay as far away from their parents as possible. She hated these kinds of parties. People unnerved her. She was trying to work on her nerves by taking the job at the strip club, but so far, nothing had happened. It was easy to talk the talk, but her hands were shaking. She held onto Riley, hoping he didn't see it, but knowing her very perceptive brother, he already knew.

From the moment they entered the house, they were swarmed by the crowd. She even spotted Landon, who made his way over.

Riley tensed up, and she truly believed they were both shocked when Landon wrapped his arms around them.

"Can you forgive me for being a total bastard?" Landon asked.

Her brother tilted his head to the side, frowning.

"I kept on hitting you. It's not part of the sport, and I shouldn't have done it." Landon held his hand out. "Forgive me."

Lou was shocked. She'd never known a Denton to actually apologize, and witnessing it now, yeah, she was in shock.

"There's our son," her mother said, shouting above the music to be heard.

She did her best to not roll her eyes, but she heard a snicker, and glanced over to see Landon chuckle. Behind him stood his brothers, who had seen her reaction as well.

"Who is this little spitfire?" Abel asked.

Lou knew all of the brothers names because Riley had made sure she knew who they were.

"My sister, my twin."

"Holy shit, you both shared a fucking womb. How did she end up the most beautiful, and you a bag of shit?" Landon asked.

It wasn't just the way he looked but also the way he talked. Lou finally understood what her brother said about Landon not seeming like a sixteen year old boy.

Before they could say anything, their mother was on Riley, pinching his cheeks and cooing over him.

Releasing her brother, Louisa folded her arms and watched the pathetic display from their parents. Looking at them, anyone would think that they loved their son when the real truth was, they had stopped him from getting a real chance in this life. It was moments like this that she had to wonder if Riley even had a clue what they had done to him.

"I see you brought your sister with you," her mother said.

"Hello, Gertrude," she said. It had been a long time since she called her "Mom".

"Louisa," Gertrude said. "What are you doing here?"

Laughing, she folded her arms. "Seeing as I was the only one there to clean up your precious son, I figured I'd come by to keep an eye on him. Make sure you're not going to turn him into a sex slave."

Riley groaned, and Lou didn't care that they had an audience. She'd seen the way Riley looked, covered in blood tonight. Their parents hadn't been there to offer him support, but they were prepared to take the credit now, and she wasn't going to allow that to happen. Riley had won tonight, not them.

"Louisa, enough!"

"Do you really think people don't see how damn false you are?"

"Aren't you supposed to be working tonight?" her father asked.

She turned to Eric, her father.

"I got the night off."

"You shouldn't be working at such a place. If you just did as you were told—"

"I could be settled down with a nice husband, being used as nothing but a damn incubator for kids, right?" She cut her mother off before she got into the flow of telling her how damn good she'd be if she just did as she was told.

Lou was done with playing by the rules, and had been when she was eighteen.

"You rude girl!"

Before long she was yelling at her mother, and her mother was yelling right back at her.

After minutes passed, Riley finally stepped between them. "Go and have a drink, Lou," he said.

"You know I'm right."

"I know, but they're never going to listen.

There's no point in wasting your breath."

"Ugh!" She walked away, not watching where she was going. People moved out of her way, which she was thankful for.

Leaving the main part of the party, she moved past the stairwell and paused. There at the top was a young girl. She had to be around ten and was so adorable with her dark brown hair and grey eyes.

"Hello," Lou said.

The girl pressed a finger to her lips, and then waved for her to come forward. The young girl was so out of place that she found herself walking upstairs. There was a time when she was the same girl sitting on the stairs, waiting, listening. Taking a seat beside the young girl, she tucked her own hair behind her ears. The young girl was wearing some teddy bear pajamas.

"Hello," she said. "I'm not allowed down there."

"How come?"

"I'm too young, and my daddy says that young girls are not allowed around his not-friends."

"Not-friends?" Lou asked.

"Friends that are not really his friends but he has to pretend like they are. He explained it to me when I was a lot younger. I'm Tamsin, by the way."

"Louisa, but my friends call me Lou."

"I like your name. It's pretty."

"Your name is pretty, too."

Tamsin wrinkled her nose. "It's not. My brothers tell me it's a boy's name all the time."

"It's not a boy's name. Don't listen to them. Boys don't know what they're talking about."

"Really?"

"Seriously, you've got to be strong, and we have to work together against them." She bumped her shoulder lightly with the young girl. Lou liked her. There was something about her that just put a smile on her face. She was still so young, and so oblivious to the world. It was refreshing to see.

"Are you trying to destroy my little sister?"

They both jumped as neither of them knew they had company. Turning around, she saw Jacob Denton leaning against the banister.

"Not at all. I'm just keeping her company."

Jacob stared at her for several seconds before turning toward Tamsin. "You, young lady, should be in bed."

Tamsin folded her arms, glaring at him. "Everyone down there is having fun."

"I'm not having fun," Lou said.

"What?" Tamsin and Jacob both asked at the same time.

"It's not all fun. Sometimes adults have to have parties for no reason but it's expected of them. What were you doing before you came sat here?"

"Reading."

"I'd love to be reading right now. A nice big mug of cocoa, there's nothing better is there?"

"No, there's not," Tamsin said.

"You better get to bed before Mom and Dad catch you."

Tamsin stuck her tongue out at her brother, giggling as she did. "It was nice to meet you, Lou."

"You, too."

She was surprised when the young girl threw her arms around her shoulders, holding onto her. "Thank you."

In the next second Tamsin was gone, and Lou was alone with Jacob.

Getting to her feet, Lou made her way back downstairs, but he stopped her by placing his hand in front of her.

"We've not been introduced," he said.

She didn't like the way he put his arm out to stop her, nor did she like how he took a step toward her.

"Louisa Moore," she said, holding her hand out, taking a step away from him. "I know who you are."

"Ah, my reputation precedes me."

She frowned. "My brother showed me your picture a few years back. That's how I know of you."

He made to reach out, and Lou flinched away from his touch. She had heard a lot of bad shit about Jacob, and she didn't even want to be alone with him.

Chapter Three

She was the most beautiful woman he'd ever seen. Jacob reached out to touch her but she flinched away from him, and in that moment, he knew that she didn't have a clue what was going on with him. From the moment he'd caught sight of her in the main room where the party was held, he'd followed her.

When he caught sight of her with his sister, he'd not been able to move. He'd been concerned for his sister as she wasn't supposed to be visible to the party members, and then he'd waited, listening to her talk. Was there a time when she was sitting on the stairs wishing she was downstairs?

"I'm not going to hurt you."

"Then why were you going to touch me?"

Lou was such a feisty woman, and nervous as hell. He wondered if she even knew it. "I was just going to tuck your hair behind your ear, Lou," he said, holding his hand up to show that he meant her no harm.

She quickly tucked her hair behind her ear. "My name is Louisa."

"I just heard you call yourself Lou with me my sister."

"I said my friends called me Lou. You're not a friend."

"Are you trying to be a bitch?"

"It comes naturally." She placed her hand on her hip, and he loved it. Jacob loved her attitude.

"So, you're Riley's twin."

"The one you didn't get to beat up."

"He held his own in the fight."

"Can I please get past?" she asked.

He shook his head. "Not at all. I'm intrigued by you."

She growled, stamping her foot. "You can't keep me here."

"I want to take you out on a date."

"No."

Jacob chuckled. She was the first woman who had ever turned him down.

"Do you know how many women there would be who'd love for me to take them out?"

"Then take them out. Go and ask them. I'm not going on a date with you."

He was about to say something else, but Riley interrupted them. "I'm heading out, sis. Do you want a ride?"

"Yes." She pushed past him before he had a chance to respond and keep her with him a few moments longer. Fuck, that one touch and he wanted more. He was fucking addicted to her already. Jacob wondered if this was what his father had gone through when he found his mother. It wasn't fun. It was a fucking nightmare. He watched her walk away from him without even a glance back.

Lou had felt nothing, and he was going to think of her as Lou, and not Louisa.

Riley placed his hand at her back, and if they were not brother and sister he'd have fucking killed the bastard for touching what belonged to him. He followed the twins out of the house, and they only stopped so that Riley could say goodbye to their parents. Lou looked everywhere else.

Only when he was sure that she was okay did he go in search of his parents. He found them both out in the garden staring up at the stars.

"He made it, baby, I told you he would."

"No more, Maddox. No more fighting."

"I can't stop the boys from fighting, but Tamsin

won't go through it."

His mother chuckled. "I don't know. The way Tamsin is, she'll demand that she gets a chance to fight."

"Not happening."

"You're not going to stop her from falling in love."

Maddox chuckled. "I'll try."

"Mom. Dad," he said, gaining their attention.

They both turned to him.

"What is it?" Charlotte asked.

"I've found my woman."

Jacob watched as his parents smiled and moved toward him. "That's awesome news. Congratulations," Maddox said.

He looked toward his mother. "She doesn't have a clue how I feel. Did you? Did you know how you felt about Dad?"

His parents shared a look, a private look that made him crazier than anything.

"Who is it?" his father asked.

"Louisa Moore."

His mother winced. "That's going to be a problem."

"Why? What's wrong with her?"

"It's not her that's the problem. Her parents are the problem. They're going to try to wrangle for a part within the family," Charlotte said. "And they're not the kind of people we want associated with us."

"You were willing to let Riley fight my brother."

"Riley was the only one willing to make the call. His parents didn't have a clue when we called to arrange the fight," Maddox said. "I've heard the twins are a good pair, but their older brothers are petty criminals. Their parents are not much better."

"I can't control the way I feel about her. I was

only close to her, and I needed to touch her, to be with her." He couldn't even begin to describe the way his feelings were consuming him. It was unlike anything he'd ever felt before. The need to follow her, to hold her was so strong, and no woman had ever made him want to do this. Sure, he liked to fuck women, and he'd screwed plenty of women in his time, but none of them had ever held him like this.

Lou hadn't even wanted him, yet he'd felt this consuming desire to claim her.

None of it made any sense to him. He didn't like it, not one bit.

"That's how it is."

"Lou had no idea. She knew who I was, but there was no feeling in her eyes or anything." He'd always assumed that his woman would feel the same as he did, yet that was turning out not to be the case.

"I never once said your woman would even realize you existed," Maddox said.

"I think I better handle this one," Charlotte said.

"I better go and have a chat with our son's future parents-in-law. Seriously? The Moores?"

"Yes."

His father walked away, shaking his head.

Charlotte chuckled. "Don't mind him. He'll get over it, or he'll keep moaning about it until he realizes that you don't have a choice."

"He knows I don't have a choice."

"He's a man, Jacob."

"How the hell does that work?"

His mother shrugged. "He's a man and he's a pain in the ass, but I love him."

Running fingers through his hair, he tried to bring some focus on what the hell was going on in his life. Jacob was used to fucking women, and forgetting them.

He wasn't used to these feelings.

"Were you in love with Dad the first moment you saw him?"

"No."

"You ended up pregnant with me young."

Charlotte smiled, and he was surprised to see the blush staining her cheeks. "I was pregnant very young with you, Jacob, but that doesn't mean I fell in love with your father."

"What the fuck does that mean?"

She glared at him. "Do not take the tone with me. I'm still your mother."

"I always assumed you and Dad were totally in love with each other."

"Me running away with you and Abel, that didn't ring any bells? Or maybe the lack of smiling photographs that we have. It took a long time for me to accept who your father was and is, and the fact that I fell in love with him over time."

"What happened?"

"When your father and I first met, I had just turned eighteen. I was young, and naive. I didn't have a clue who he was when he approached me in a bar over thirty-five years ago. My friends knew who he was, and they couldn't believe that I snagged this hot guy. I was the chubby girl of the group, but Maddox, he didn't look at any other woman." Charlotte smiled. "I'd never been with a guy, and most of the time they passed me by because of my weight. They didn't want a fat girl."

Even now, Jacob wanted to go back and hurt those bastards for hurting his mother. He was very protective of his mother, sister, and all of his brothers. Jacob had certainly gotten into a lot of fights to finish the beat down that his brothers were getting.

"Anyway, that night, Maddox treated me like a

princess. He bought me drinks, dinner, and we danced. We danced long into the night, and yeah, it was magical, but I also knew it wasn't going to last. When we went back to his place, we did the business that meant we could have you." Charlotte sighed. "I didn't know I was going to get pregnant, so I snuck out the next morning. I didn't see Maddox for three months until he discovered me coming out of an adoption agency."

This was all news to him.

"Adoption? You were going to give me up?"

"At first, yes. It was a different world back then, and I discovered I was pregnant, and I didn't have a clue how to get in touch with Maddox. My friends wouldn't tell me who he was, and so, I felt I had no choice. I was coming out of the adoption agency because I decided I couldn't do it. I couldn't give up my baby. Even before I gave birth to you, Jacob, I loved you."

"What happened?" The revelations tonight were scaring the shit out of him. He always assumed that when he found the woman destined to be his, she'd feel the same way, and now his parents were telling him differently.

"I discovered who Maddox was, what the Denton name meant, and that I was now about to become his wife. I didn't really have a say in what was going on, and I was afraid. I was pregnant with a man I had one amazing night with, and after that, it felt like I was living a nightmare. Maddox, he was always sweet and charming, but it was hard. That man I found sweet and charming dealt with women, drugs, guns, crime, all of it. I was just a small town girl who wanted to become a nurse, to help people. Maddox, he was the very opposite of the person I was. The biggest problem was when he was away, it was easy to remember who he was. When he was near, I forgot. Not once did he change, or raise a hand to me, or even get angry with me." Charlotte's eyes were wet with tears. "I just couldn't handle it."

"What made you fall in love with him?"

"Time. It took time, and a lot of chocolate, kids, and time."

"Time?"

"Yeah, time."

"How much time?" he asked.

"There's not a limit on love, honey." His mother tapped his cheek. "You've just got to give it time."

That was not an answer he wanted.

****

"Your brother did good last night I heard," Ben, the barman at the strip club, said.

"Yeah, he did. Got banged around as well."

"Landon is a tough guy. All the Denton men are tough guys."

Lou stared at Ben. He'd asked her out a couple of times, and she had declined as nicely as she could. They were friends, and he was currently dating one of the strippers. She didn't know how that was going to go, but he never acted jealous when the girl was dancing. People and relationships were completely strange to her.

"Wow, I didn't even know you knew a Denton," she said.

"Everyone knows who they are. They're the biggest crime family in the world."

"Great. Crime family and you sound totally in awe of them."

Ben sighed. "You don't understand at all. The Dentons are dangerous yet fair. They're completely crazy, and people always underestimate them as a family at first."

"Why?"

"Something about the men being head over heels

in love. Their enemies seem to think that being in love is in some way a huge sin. It's not."

She rolled her eyes as he gazed down her body, landing on her breasts. Part of working in a strip club meant her tits were pressed together, and on show. Fortunately, she'd been allowed to wear pants, but they were the kind that pinched in at the waist giving her an hourglass figure even if her ass and stomach were well rounded. She was never going on a diet again. She probably should, but that wasn't going to happen today.

"My eyes are up here," she said.

"Can't blame a guy for loving a nice pair of tits. What would it take to have yours swinging in front of my face as you ride my cock?" He reached over, stroking a finger down her arm.

"It's never going to happen, sweetie." She took hold of his hand, moving it back to his space. "Let's not get grabby."

Ben sighed. "Baby, you hurt me."

"You'll get over it."

She watched as he finished her order, placing drinks on her serving tray.

"The Dentons come in every now and again. Not often but when they do, the women go crazy. They're great tippers, and they're great for business. Frank is friends with them, and so they stop by every now and again."

In the last year that she had been there, they hadn't. "I've never seen them."

"You've not been working the nights they have. The women though, they tend to need the next day off to recuperate."

"Why?"

Ben chuckled. "They're known for fucking women until they're sore."

"In the club?"

"Yep, wherever they go, and there's always a party with them. They tip well, and they have fun while they do it. Enjoy."

She took the tray, annoyed that he'd made her more curious than anything. "When was the last time they were here?"

"You called in sick about two months ago, and that's when they came in last."

Lou remembered. She'd been so sick, and it had been hard for her to get out of the bathroom with vomiting. In the end she'd had to call Riley to come and help. She asked her mother, but she hadn't wanted anything to do with her, so the only person left was her brother. Lou avoided her other brothers as they would only try to steal the stuff she'd managed to get over the years.

All her life it had been her and Riley.

Taking the tray, she delivered the order to the table of businessmen, making sure she didn't cut their view of the woman on stage. She didn't know who it was today, a new starter or something. The woman didn't look older than nineteen but her tits were huge, and she was doing everything in her power to show the men how damn dirty she could be.

This kind of club also allowed the women to put on little sex shows if they wanted. There were even rooms in the back for the girls to make a little extra on the side. Frank had even given her a key. Whatever they made in the back had to be given to him, and he'd split the money. She'd handed him the key straight back, telling him not a chance in hell.

For some reason, Frank had said he liked her spirit, and he needed a woman who was determined to stay on the straight and narrow. Whatever that meant.

Either way, she was never going to a back room, and she had seen most of the strippers use it to make extra cash.

There was one girl, Susan, who had a little girl, and had told her that it was the easiest way in the world to make money. There was no thought to it. All she had to do was do some moaning and groaning to make sure the man was happy with his performance. Half of the time she was thinking about what to do for her kid the next day.

Once she was done, Lou moved away and gritted her teeth as one of the guys touched her ass.

She hated it when they thought they could grab her. Moving around the busy room, she worked for another twenty minutes supplying drinks and serving up some finger foods. When no one wanted her, she moved away, and stood in the corner, keeping an eye on the room.

"I thought you were going to beat the shit out of that man," Frank said.

Lou turned surprised to see that her boss was sitting at the end of the bar, watching her. "Do you want me to get you a drink?"

"Not at all, sugar. Ben fixed me up, but I wanted to come out and see the action." He nodded toward the girl on stage.

"I don't know her name."

"Trixie, she says, but I doubt that's her real name. Women think they can stay anonymous by changing their name. They can't change how they look."

"That they can't."

"Come and sit with me."

Placing her serving tray on the counter, she took a seat, looking out at the room. "This is a good angle. You can see everything." She pushed some hair off her face and turned back to him.

"Like I saw that guy grabbing your ass."

She chuckled. "I figured you wouldn't want the lawsuit if I was to hit him with my serving tray."

"True, it would piss me off, but then I'd get a thrill out of seeing a woman beat the shit out of him."

Laughing along with him, she declined the offer of a drink. In an environment like this, she had to keep her focus on.

"Water it is then."

"I'll take a water." She smiled at Ben as he put her drink in front of her.

"I heard about your brother."

"Everyone has heard about my brother it would seem."

"He's a good man, and he did well. You should be proud."

She took a sip of her drink and nodded. "I am proud. He's still my brother, and I never want to see him get hurt. Fighting at venues like that, it's dangerous, and he's my brother. I'm sure you can understand my fear for him."

"I get it, and I even understand it."

Biting her lip, she looked toward the businessmen. When she'd first started working at the strip club, to rub her parents up the wrong way, she thought the businessmen would be the most civilized in places like this. They were not. They were the worst kind of pigs out there. "I'm surprised you let you bar open to them."

Frank laughed. "Honey, there's always different ways to deal with assholes like that. You see, honey, those men are paying double the going rate for all the drinks. You ever wonder why I don't keep a display for the drinks and prices? I can charge whatever the fuck I want to."

"I also heard a rumor that cops come here, but I've not seen anyone here."

"You have, honey, believe me, you have. You've just not seen them. They're not always dressed in proper uniform. When they want to fuck around with me, they come dressed in uniform." Frank pulled out a cigarette, and she watched him spark up. She wasn't interested in smoking, and she did her best to smile and ignore it. His club. His rules.

"Tell your brother when he next comes by he can have the night for free, drinks, girls, you name it."

"I'll be sure to let him know, and make sure I'm not here when he does. We're related, but I don't care to see him that up close and personal." She wrinkled her nose and got to her feet. The businessmen table needed serving once again.

Frank let her go, and as she was collecting glasses from the table, the main doors opened, and a loud array of male hollers and whistles were heard throughout the small party. Turning toward the door, she froze as she watched the Denton boys with her brother come into the club.

Great! She didn't catch sight of Landon, which she was pleased about. The last thing she wanted was to cause a problem by refusing to serve a minor. Denton or not, she was not breaking any laws, and especially knowing that cops frequented the club.

She finished grabbing the empty glasses, avoided spanker's hands, and made her way toward the bar. At the same time, the large party took three tables, and they were not all Dentons either. Her brother was there, and she didn't recognize the other guys. Frank walked toward their table, and she heard the crowd go wild.

"Ben, anything at this table, free, you got me," Frank said, shouting for Ben to here.

"I got it." He held his hand up in a wave, and turned back to her. "Wow, it must be your lucky night."

"My lucky night?"

"You were asking about the Dentons."

"No. You were talking, and I just made you keep on talking about them." She gave him a wink. He finished her tray, and she left him alone to keep on serving. Before she had a chance to move away from the bar, she turned, and was stopped by a very large masculine chest.

Pausing, she glanced up to find Jacob stood in front of her.

"Hello," she said.

That's all you can think to say? Hello.

You don't like him, remember?

Her mind was having one of those brain farts where she didn't have a clue what to do.

"You work at a strip club. Riley told us you did, but I had to say, I didn't believe him."

She glanced toward her brother to see that he was a little drunk.

"What are you doing?"

Fear gripped her as she looked toward the one person she loved more than anything. She had a connection with Riley whereas she didn't have with the rest of her family. Lou relied on him, cared for him.

"What's wrong?" he asked.

She never once thought that her brother was in danger, yet looking at Jacob, and then over at her brother, her stomach started to tighten. "Are you going to hurt him?"

Chapter Four

Jacob saw the fear in her eyes, and he looked toward Riley, not understanding what her problem was at first. Then, when he looked at it from an innocent's pair of eyes, he understood.

"We're not going to do anything to him."

"Why are you here with Riley?"

"We decided to take him out, have a drink. Usually we all do it after a fight, but Landon is in trouble, and he's staying at home."

Lou laughed, but it wasn't the natural kind. It was filled with hysteria. "Riley was at the gym tonight."

"You work in a strip club?"

"As you can see."

He did see. Her tits were pressed together and almost spilling out of the tight shirt. The pants she wore molded to her curves, and he had to give Frank credit, he knew how to dress a woman.

"You look very nice." Staring at her all he wanted to do was take her in his arms, and as far away from this place as possible. Instead, he kept remembering his mother's words. He had to work to earn her trust, her love. She didn't feel this need that he did.

"Thanks. So, erm, you're intending to party?" she asked, glancing over once again at her brother. She also bit her lip, and he wanted to bite that lip for her.

"We're not going to hurt your brother. I have a lot of respect for him."

"Considering he agreed to fight a kid?"

"My brother is not just any kid." He was about to rest his hand on his hips but stopped when he remembered the gun strapped to his body. Jacob never went anywhere without being heavily armed. "We're here to celebrate as we accept Riley into the fold."

"The fold?"

"He's going to be working with me as a partner."

"What do you do?" she asked.

"Stuff." He never talked about his business. His father was the head of the business, and he took orders from him, from their main business in the center of the city, a casino. It was so fucking cliché, but his father had a head for numbers, and with casinos, they could be built over the country, and even abroad. It's an easy way to get the feds to look the other way while the real business went down. He did everything his father told him to. Yes, he hurt people, and he'd killed people for his family. Staring at Lou, he just knew she wasn't ready to deal with that kind of shit. Then he had a horrible feeling. What if she was never ready to deal with that kind of stuff?

"Stuff?"

"I do a lot of stuff."

"Okay, well my mother always told me not to ask too many questions, and I guess it's one of those moments. I've got work to do."

She pushed past him, making her way toward the table of businessmen. He didn't like the way they looked at her.

"What can I get you?" Ben asked. "Do you want me to call the women out to party?"

Jacob returned his attention to the barman. He liked Ben, and this had been the place he and his brothers could let off steam. They all loved fucking, and the women at the strip club were always more than happy to give them what they wanted. If he wanted his dick sucked, all he had to do was pull it out, and suck away she would.

He gave the table order and made his way back to where his brothers were laughing and joking. Jacob took a seat beside Riley, and watched Lou as he did. The businessmen were screaming at the stripper on stage who was giving them all a show of her cunt and ass.

Lou avoided their groping hands, and Jacob gritted his teeth in the hope of keeping all of his senses. He was so damn angry, and he wanted to kill every motherfucker who tried to touch her.

"Your sister doesn't like me," he said.

Riley snorted. "She doesn't like a lot of people. You know she's only working here to piss our mother off."

"Why?"

"Do you like my sister?"

The whole table had gone quiet.

"Why does she want to piss your mother off?"

Riley's drunken expression changed, and Jacob was even surprised by the sudden change in the man. He'd been faking it, and Jacob developed a lot of respect for Riley. Unlike most of the Moores, Riley wasn't out for everything he could get. "What do you want to do with my sister?"

"I want to fuck her!" Jacob leaned in close. "But before I fuck her, I want to take her out on a date."

"You fucker!" Riley went to grab him, but Jacob's brothers kept him down in his seat. He fought though, and the rest of his men formed a barricade around them. "You're not coming near my sister."

Jacob sighed. "Stop fighting. I've got no intention of ever hurting your sister. Have you heard the rumors about the Denton men?"

"What?"

"The Denton men, the legacy, and the shit around our women?"

"Some rumor that you only love once, and you're possessive as fuck when it comes to your woman.

Everyone has heard that fucking rumor. Your father doesn't exactly hide how he fucking feels."

Riley stopped straining, but Jacob didn't call off his brothers. Abel and Oliver held Riley down, straining to keep the strong man seated. Jacob didn't want to cause a fuss in front of Lou.

"It's the truth, and your sister belongs to me."

Several seconds passed, and confusion crossed Riley's face before he finally relaxed. "Belongs to you?"

"Up until three days ago I had to say I didn't believe the rumors about the family men of our line. Seeing Louisa, I knew she was meant for me."

"You want to date my sister?" Riley asked.

"I want to date her. I want her to get used to me being around, and then I'm going to marry her."

Riley shook his head. "I can't help you with that shit. Is that why you came to see me? Why I made it to being your partner?"

"No. You earned being my partner all on your own. My father was already going to give you that shot. Tonight, I wanted to get a chance to find out more about your sister. Now, why is she working at a strip club?"

"I told you. She's trying to piss our mother off. Lou isn't like other women in this world, and she intends to stand on her own two feet. She's not going to be pushed around, or ordered."

"I have no intention of ordering her around." Apart from in the bedroom, but he doubted Riley wanted to know about that.

"Mom tried to marry her off to some Italian guy who comes to the gym. He's rich and gets his kicks out of betting on the underground fights. That's why Lou changed jobs. Before this she was some receptionist at a law firm." Riley stared at him, assessing. "If you hurt her, I'll break your fucking neck."

Jacob leaned in close. "From what I've been told, if I hurt her, I'll be hurting myself."

"You Dentons are creepy as fuck! Anyone ever told you that?"

"Probably," he said, laughing. "You're not the first one to think it."

"And you're not the first one to assume it either," Abel said.

They all calmed down, and took a seat.

Riley glanced over to Lou, who was watching them.

"She's a good woman," Frank said. "I like her. I was going to try her out myself, but I think I'll bow out of that one, and leave it to you."

Jacob turned his attention back to Frank. "What the fuck?"

Frank held his hands up. "I'm a guy, and I love to fuck. She's a pretty little thing, and she doesn't even have a clue how damn beautiful she is. It makes a guy want to show her how special she is."

"You keep her safe, but you keep your hands to yourself, do you hear me?"

"I won't be poaching on your territory." Frank held his hands up again. "Does she know what you've got planned for her?"

"Hey, guys," Lou said, interrupting them. She held a tray of drinks, and there were too many there. "I'm really sorry, but can you guys grab what you need to? There's a lot here." Her body was tense as she held all the drinks, and he gritted his teeth looking over at the bar. Ben was too busy chatting up a blonde to even care. Jacob was going to have to have a word about that. He didn't want his woman hurting. "Do I need to stick around to drive you home?" she asked.

"Nah, I'm good. I'm staying here and party."

Lou looked a little disgusted. "I heard about the last party you had. If I'm still working with you take that, you know, to one of the rooms? The last thing I want to see is my brother in that kind of—yeah, I'm not even going to go there."

She didn't look embarrassed, and Riley laughed. "You're still scared from the time I took Becky to my room, and you walked in."

"You didn't even put a sock or a condom on the door handle. That kind of stuff is not acceptable."

"It was my bedroom."

"I don't care. It was my eyes that nearly went blind from seeing your naked ass and balls." Lou shuddered. "I'll leave you gentlemen to your drinks."

"Speaking of our last party, where are the women?" Gideon asked.

Jacob sat back as Frank went to get the women. The last party he was part of, he'd shared two girls with Abel. Tonight, he wasn't going to be looking at any other woman. Lou held his attention with the way her curvy ass leaned over the table. The businessmen were getting loud, and hollering all kinds of shit at the girl on stage. Their noise was starting to piss him off.

When Lou took them over a drink, he watched as she caught around the waist, and forced to sit down. Jacob didn't take time to assess. He got out of his chair, and stormed over to the table. He listened to his brothers call his name. The one who had caught Lou rubbed his hand between her thighs, and tried to capture her mouth. Lou was trying to fight, but the way he held her, her arms were trapped.

Rage consumed him as they touched his woman.

"Let her go," Jacob said. If he shot the bastard there was a risk he'd hit her.

The man looked up at him. "Go and find your

own slut."

Wrong answer.

Lou had frozen into place, and he grabbed his knife out of his pocket, throwing it at the man's shoulder. He screamed, releasing Lou, and Jacob grabbed her, giving her to her brother, even though he didn't want to.

"It's time you learned some fucking respect," Jacob said.

****

Sitting inside Frank's office, Lou wrapped her arms around herself while Riley knelt in front of her.

"Are you with me, Lou?"

She nodded. For the past year she'd been working in the strip club and never once had she been treated like that. Her heart raced, and she felt so damn dirty. Tears filled her eyes and before she could stop them, they were falling. She was so damn scared, and she wasn't used to the feeling. "I'm not okay."

"Do you feel happy getting back at Mom?"

"What?" she asked. This was not the time for that kind of conversation. "You're seriously going to ask me that."

"Fuck, Lou, some bastard has just mauled you right in front of me, and before I could get to you, Jacob fucking Denton did." Riley got to his feet, and to her shame she couldn't hold the tears back.

She heard the masculine scream of pain, and she shuddered.

"Calm down, Riley. This wasn't your sister's fault," Frank said.

"What about you? You let assholes like that inside your fucking club, touching my sister up?"

"Enough!" Lou said, screaming out. "What's done is done." She was shaking like mad, and Riley wasn't helping her feel any better. "Please, just either calm down, or leave. I don't need this right now."

She'd never been touched in such a way unless she was actually asking for it.

Minutes passed, and finally Riley knelt in front of her. "Shit, honey, I'm so sorry. I just went a little crazy. What do you want me to do?"

"Nothing. Not to say horrible things like you did about Mom. Yeah, I work here to spite her, but I happen to also like working here, too. Most of the time I'm safe here. Frank, he's a good boss. This is the first inciden—"

"Those fuckers are gone, and they're not coming back."

Lou turned to find Jacob in the doorway. He looked crazed, which only startled her even more.

Without another word, he walked in, moving Riley aside as he knelt in front of her. "Are you okay? Did that bastard hurt you?"

He made to reach out to her, but she spotted the blood on his hands and froze up. She hated the sight of blood.

Jacob paused, staring at his hands. "They won't be hurting you again."

She didn't know what the hell to make of what he'd done for her. There was no doubt that he had hurt the guy who touched her.

"Do you have somewhere I can wash up?"

Frank opened another door showing a small bathroom.

"You can go out and enjoy your party," Lou said. She didn't want Riley to miss out on his fun.

"No, I'm not going to do that."

"Why? Look, you were having fun, and I'm fine. You know me, and I don't like to have an audience. I've already overreacted."

"No."

"Riley, honestly, I'm fine." She smiled up at him, trying her best to appear strong.

"I think it's best that Louisa takes the rest of the night off," Frank said. "I'll make sure she gets home."

"No need. I'll deal with her," Jacob said. "I'll make sure she gets home safely, and I know a diner that serves late. I'll feed her as well."

"That's not necessary."

"I wasn't asking," Jacob said.

She gritted her teeth, hating the way he was being bossy. The last thing she wanted was to spend time with him, but she also refused to spoil Riley's night.

"Are you sure?"

"I'm more than sure. Go, have fun, and enjoy your night. I imagine you're going to be like super busy soon."

Riley stared at her for several seconds.

"Go," she said.

"I love you, little sis."

"I'm only a few minutes younger than you."

"Those few minutes count. Call me when you get home."

"I will." She watched Riley leave the office, and Frank made his excuses to leave. When they were gone, she slumped in her chair, and just gave up to the fear that was consuming her.

Jacob gripped her arm, and she tensed, crying out. Quickly moving out of his reach, she turned to face him, shaking.

He held his hands up. "I'm not going to hurt you."

She wiped away the tears that were refusing to stop falling. Lou hadn't cried in so long.

"You hurt him?" she asked.

"Yes. He put his hands on you, and now I wished

I hadn't let him walk out here alive. He's made you cry."

She bit her lip, trying to contain her emotions. It was hard with Jacob staring at her as if he could see right into her soul.

"Have you killed people before?"

"Do you want me to lie to you or pretend?"

"I want the truth."

Jacob's jaw tensed up as she watched him grit his teeth. "Go out on a date with me."

"What?" She frowned.

"Go out on a date with me, and I will answer any and all questions you want."

Lou didn't know what to think. "If I say no?"

"I don't give you a single answer, and you won't have a clue what Riley is up to."

"Will you kill someone in front of me?"

He smirked.

"Why are you smirking?" she asked.

"You know, we've been talking for a couple of minutes and you've stopped shaking. I'd say I was good for your health."

"You're not good for my health. You're an asshole."

Jacob closed the distance between them, and Lou had no choice but to take a step back. He kept advancing, and she kept backing away until finally her back was against the wall. His hand moved above her head, and the jacket he wore couldn't hide the thick, corded muscles in his arms. Biting her lip, she tried not to show her fear, and a little arousal as well. No man had ever done something like this with her before, chased her. That was what Jacob made her feel, chased. In a weird way, he made her feel special.

"I've hurt men for calling me less," he said.

"Less what?"

"Less than an asshole. I'm not a very nice person."

"I know that. You've killed people?"

"Go on a date with me."

Lou tilted her head to the side, forcing herself to keep looking him in the eye. She shook her head. "No."

He leaned in close so that his lips were touching her ear. "Are you a chicken?"

Jerking back, she placed her hands against his chest. "I'm not going on a date with you. It'll just give you an excuse not to tell me the truth."

"Or maybe I'll show you too much truth. Your parents, they're not good people."

"I know that."

"No, you don't. You know what you think you know."

Her heart started to pound. "You'd take me with you? No hiding?"

"No hiding, but you've got to promise me you won't run to the cops."

Lou frowned. "Why take me around if you risk me going to the cops?"

He twirled a strand of her hair between his fingers, and the back of his knuckles brushed along her cheek. She tensed up, not knowing what he was going to do. Jacob was confusing to her. Lou didn't want to give him anything, and yet he was determined to take. He annoyed her.

"You want something, to know the truth about your brother, and what he's doing. I'm willing to give you the answer you want."

"And in return?"

"You go on a date with me. It will be a combined date of knowing what I do, and having dinner with me."

Gritting her teeth, she saw that he had her interest

piqued, which only annoyed her.

"What is it going to be?" he asked.

Several seconds passed until she finally caved. Her parents wouldn't let her know anything, and she was always left in the dark about what they did. She knew they operated the illegal fights, but that was it.

"Yes, I'll go on a date with you."

"Wednesday night," he said.

"Why then?"

"Because your brother doesn't start until Thursday, and it's the night I've got free. Now, let's take you home." He grabbed her arm, and together they made their way out of the strip club. Before she left, she looked over his arm to find all the strippers out and dancing for the men. When she caught sight of her brother sucking a woman's breasts, she winced, and turned back to the front.

"Someone ever told you that curiosity killed the cat?" he asked.

"How did you know what I saw?"

"I didn't. I guessed."

She wrinkled her nose. "I didn't take my car tonight. I walked."

Jacob paused, glaring down at her. "You walked?"

"Yes."

"What the fuck! Do you know how fucking dangerous this place is at night?"

"I'm not in the mood to be badgered. Are you taking me for food or not?"

Jacob opened the door, and they made their way out into the warm night air.

"From now on, you either come by car, or you call me."

"Not happening. I've agreed to go on one date.

That's all. I'm not going to have my life invaded by yours."

Jacob caught her arm and pressed her up against his car. At least, she assumed it was his car. "Are you going to be a pain in my ass all the time?"

"Maybe."

He pressed his body against hers, and she struggled to think of a reason as to why he shouldn't be touching her. One of his hands gripped her arm, and the other touched her waist. Her heart was pounding.

She didn't mean to be a pain in the ass, but it was so damn easy to be a bitch. It was easier never to expect anything from anyone, so she was never disappointed. Growing up, she'd been disappointed her whole life, from Christmas to parents, to parties. She had learned at a young age that her parents were not like others. The best way to protect herself was by not letting anyone get close. It sucked, but it worked.

"You were nice to my sister, Lou."

"It's Louisa."

"And I think there's more to you than you let anyone see. Riley, he was talking about how damn sweet you are, and yet, you've been nothing but a bitch to me." Jacob smiled, gripping her hip a little tighter. "I think I'm looking forward to finding that sweet woman you hide from the world."

He released her, easing her away from the door, and opening it up. "Let's go and have some food."

Chapter Five

Taking a seat in the booth opposite Lou, Jacob couldn't look away. She was a beautiful woman, no doubt about that. He loved her green eyes, and the way they kept looking at everything but at him. Jacob wondered what she was thinking. She reached out, picking up the menu and opening it up. Her blonde hair looked a mess where it was bound at the back.

"Release your hair," he said. He wished to see those blonde locks falling all around her.

"What?" She lowered her menu, frowning at him.

"Your hair, release it."

The pulse at the side of her neck started to pound. They were only subtle changes, and he had to wonder if she even realized that she was attracted to him.

"Are you crazy?"

Jacob sat back, staring at her. "I'll take you to the casino to meet my father, and you can see where we do business." She didn't need to know that he had every intention of showing her everything. He wasn't going to hide who he was, and he saw that with Lou, he'd have to be open and honest.

"You'd do that? Doesn't that break some kind of Denton rule?"

He shook his head. "Take your hair down."

"If I don't?"

"You don't get to see it."

"Ugh! See? You had no intention of showing me shit."

When she made to move, he pressed his leg against her seat and grabbed her arm, applying a little pressure. He didn't try to hurt her, just enough to make her stop.

"I'm going to show you a great deal. You're not

part of the family. I'm offering you a deal to go out with me."

"You're not making any sense at all."

"Good. Take your hair down, and you're going to have to learn to trust me."

"You're doing this on purpose?"

"What? Tempting you? Making you want something you didn't think you wanted to know?" he asked.

"Yes to everything, and you're doing it on purpose."

Leaning forward, he captured her chin, running his thumb across her bottom lip. He was a little surprised that she didn't try to bite him. "Let's just say I know what I need to do to make sure you belong to me."

"This is not going to get you in my pants."

"You will, when the time is right." His cock was rock hard, and he was finding it hard not to just grab her, bend her over the nearest counter, and fuck her. But he wasn't into rape, and Lou wasn't going to give in easily.

"You arrogant ass."

"I know, and you're going to love it about me." He gave her a wink. "Do we have a deal?"

She sighed, and pulled her hair out, letting it fall down.

Letting her go, he sat back. "Run your fingers through your hair," he said.

Lou ran fingers through her hair doing as he instructed. "There? Are you satisfied?"

"Yes, I am." Handing her the menu, he urged her to order. "Pick whatever you want."

"Do you own this place as well?"

"The Dentons own everything."

She shook her head. "You know the rumors about you are not good."

"What kind of rumors?" he asked, intrigued. There were a lot of rumors about him and his family.

"That you're not known for showing mercy."

"Yet you don't know if I've killed anyone."

She shrugged. "I try not to listen to rumors, but seeing as we're here, I figured it's a good point of talking about something."

"Do you really think we've not got anything in common?" he asked.

"No. We're completely different. There's no way we have anything in common." She looked up from the menu.

Running a finger across his bottom lip, he watched her. He wanted to see those full tits bouncing in front of his face as he rode her pussy hard. "Are you a virgin?"

She rested her arms on the table, placing the menu in front of them. "Are you?"

"A little fighter. I like it. No, I'm not a virgin. I like pussy way too much."

"I'm not a virgin either."

"Really?"

"Why do you sound so surprised?" she asked.

"Your parents—"

She laughed. "Yeah, my parents. They're the reason I've made so many crazy decisions, and I've hated most of them. My virginity, I gave it up when I realized that my parents were looking for a prospective husband for me." She snorted, and he saw the pain in her eyes. "I was seventeen at the time, and I wasn't interested in sex and fucking. I was walking downstairs in our home when I overheard them talking to some guy. I don't know who he was, but they were saying how I'd never been with a boy, not even had a boyfriend or something like that. Anyway, to cut a long story short, he wanted a virgin bride, and I was a virgin. By the end of the week, I was no longer a virgin." Her hands shook a little as she picked up her menu. "I'm in the mood for greasy. What about you?"

He looked down at his menu, angry at her parents. This was the world where they lived, and most of the time, women were married off as some kind of trophy. He shouldn't be angry, but he was. He was fucking furious.

"You didn't want to have sex?" he asked.

She looked up from her menu. "As shocking as this may sound, I wasn't actually ready to give it up. I did it because I felt that if I didn't do something, they were going to take the decision right out of my hands, and that I couldn't stomach. This is my life, my body." She forced another laugh. "I say those words, and yet I fucked a guy I didn't like because he was easy, and I knew he'd brag about bagging the Moore girl. Riley beat the shit out of the guy, which again didn't make me happy. When I think of my life, all I see is a bunch of decisions that were taken out of my hands."

"Is that why you don't want to go on a date with me?"

Lou licked her lips. "It's one of them. Besides, I don't want to be part of this life, this world that you Dentons rule."

"Have you fucked a man you wanted to?"

She nodded. "Yes, a couple of years ago. I'm not a prude. When was the first time you had sex?"

"I was thirteen, and I seduced the babysitter. She was eighteen."

Lou's eyes grew wide.

"You didn't think I was going to tell you who I've screwed?"

"Trying to get a date with a woman doesn't start

out by telling that woman who you've fucked before."

"I figured out early on that you're not like any other woman. I'm going to be upfront with you."

"Interesting," she said.

"Can I help you with anything?" a waitress asked, interrupting their conversation.

"I'd like your burger with everything on it," Lou said. "Don't skip anything. I'm not going to be on a diet today."

After she ordered, Jacob watched as she looked across the diner, clocking his guards. Jacob was a strong man, and he'd take whatever was thrown at him, but he was also the oldest son of a Denton. His father wouldn't let him go anywhere without a guard.

Once he finished ordering, he waited for Lou to return her attention to him.

"Those two men are watching you," she said.

"They're paid to watch me."

"Oh, bodyguards."

"Yes."

"So, have you ever been married?" she asked.

"No."

"This business requires you to marry well, right?"

He shook his head. "I'll marry who I want to marry, and I won't be told before then."

"Must be nice to have that kind of control."

"You don't think you have?"

"I can work in shitty jobs, and piss my parents off, but at the end of the day, they're the ones who always have the control."

"Who?"

"My brother, Riley. They like to put him in circumstances to keep me in line."

"Why were you at the fight the other day?"

"My parents weren't going to be there, and I

heard who he was fighting. I care about my brother, Jacob. He's the only family I have, and I love him very much."

They paused as the waitress brought them out their drinks order. He had a strong coffee while she had a milkshake.

"This work you're taking him out on, it's dangerous, right? More dangerous than getting into a fight?"

"The fights can sometimes be to the death, you know that?"

"I know that. Riley, he doesn't fight to the death. He told me he doesn't."

"And you believe him?"

"I've got no reason to doubt him."

Riley had lied to her. Jacob had seen Riley fight, and he'd watched Riley kill his opponent. This was not his confession to make.

"I'm not going to lie and say the work isn't dangerous. It is. Please be reassured that I'm the one going to be there by his side. I'll keep him safe."

"Do you promise?"

"I promise."

The waitress came back to the table with their food. "This looks really good."

He watched as Lou grabbed her burger and took a huge bite.

"Wow, just wow, that is so amazing," she said.

"I told you this was a good place."

"And to think I wasn't going to take you up on that date."

"Ah, you admit you'll go on a date with me?"

She shrugged. "I've not got anything else to do. I may as well have some fun with you." She gave him a wink, and Jacob relished the small victory. He wasn't fucking her yet, but he would.

****

"Once you've vetted my boss will you give me permission to work for him?" Riley asked.

Lou glanced over at her brother, who had stopped by while she'd been getting ready to go out on her date. "I'm not vetting your boss."

"You screw him and I'd probably get a raise."

She rolled her eyes. "Will you stop? The only way you'll be getting a raise is if you work damned hard."

"I know that, but Jacob has a thing for you."

"Please stop."

"He's asked you out on a date, and he pretty much had to tempt that curiosity of yours before you'd give in."

Lou shrugged. "Nothing is going to happen."

"No? Wow, think of how much the parentals would love you."

"Stop it, Riley."

Her brother held his hands up. "I'm just, you know, putting it out there for you."

"I'd rather you didn't. This is not about them, and I'm not going to let them spoil it by thinking it is."

"You've got issues. You know that, right?" Riley asked.

"I'm already a nervous wreck. The last thing I need to be thinking about right now is my parents. Now," she ran her hands down her legs, "how do I look?" She turned to her brother.

"Cute."

"Cute?"

"Isn't that what you were going for?"

"I was going for practical."

"Practical? You're going on a date."

"Oh, I hate you!" She wore a pair of jeans and a white blouse. On her feet she wore a slender heel that gave her a little more height. She doubted he'd allow her to see the real dangerous element of his life, so she'd gone for the practical look. She wasn't the kind of woman who needed expensive restaurants.

The jeans also give you an added layer of protection.

She hated to admit it, but Jacob Denton was in fact a nice looking man. No, nice looking didn't even begin to cover it. He was fucking hot, and she hadn't been with a man in so long. The night where he'd taken her for dinner had been fun, even if she remembered the night with a bit of a shudder. Jacob had made it fun, and after food, he'd taken her home.

"No, you don't hate me. You love me."

"Why are you here?"

"I wanted to see that you were all right. I was an awful brother. I left Jacob to take care of you, and I felt bad about it."

"You were enjoying your party."

"It was a good party."

The sound of her bell ringing interrupted them, and she sighed. Her hands were shaking as moved to the door. Gripping the handle, she pulled the door open, and there stood Jacob. He was dressed in a suit, and he looked damn good. It was a black suit with a crisp white shirt peeking out. He looked every part the businessman.

"Hello," she said.

"You look beautiful."

No man had ever called her beautiful before.

"Thank you."

"I will see myself out," Riley said. "I hope you both have a good night."

"I'll be by to pick you up at three tomorrow

afternoon. I expect you to be ready."

"And I'll be waiting."

Riley winked at her before leaving. Heat filled her cheeks, and she invited Jacob into her small apartment. "It's not much, but it is home," she said.

"I like it."

Locking her fingers together, she watched him as he stared at her house. She wasn't freaking out at all. *Complete and total lie.* She was freaking out.

"Thank you."

"Are you ready to go?" he asked.

"Yes. I am."

She already had some cash in her back pocket in case she needed it. Grabbing some keys, she headed for the door, and waited for him.

Jacob looked around her apartment, taking everything in. "You're nervous about me being in your space?"

"Not at all."

His hands were inside his pants, and she couldn't help but notice how his suit seemed to bulge over his arms.

"Don't you want to get started?" Her pussy was having other ideas, and she wanted to strip naked and put her virgin mattress to some use.

"Lead the way."

Opening her apartment door, she waited for him to exit before closing up. Pocketing her keys, and followed beside him. When they got onto the elevator, she found that she couldn't look away from him.

"Do you have any questions about tonight?" he asked.

"None at all." She was just going to see how the night went. "Will I be allowed to ask questions as the night goes on?"

"Yeah, so long as I can ask them of you as well."

"Okay, cool." Questions she could handle. "How old are you?"

"Thirty-five. You?"

"Twenty-five, but you knew that already."

"I did, but still, I just wanted to make sure that you understood the rules."

She took a deep breath. "I get it."

The doors pinged open, and they walked out of the doors together. Jacob placed a hand at her back, and she found herself closing her eyes at his touch. Before she fell flat on her face, she pushed those feelings aside. There was no way she intended to fall for this man.

Within seconds they were inside his car, and Jacob turned to her.

He leaned over, opening the glove compartment.

Lou released a little squeal as she watched him grab out a gun, which looked like a Glock.

"What the hell?"

"Tonight is going to be dangerous. Do you know how to work a gun?"

Since she'd left her parents' house, Riley made sure she could take care of herself. "Yes."

"Good. Take it with you tonight. I don't care where you have to store it, but I want you to keep it on your person."

"Can't you store it?"

"If shit goes down, you need to be able to get it."

"Fuck!" Her heart raced. Fear gripped her.

"You wanted this, remember? If you just want to have dinner, I can make that happen."

"No. I'm good."

"You're crazy. Most women just want an expensive dinner, some jewels, and a good long fuck."

"I take it you give them what they want?"

"Most of the time."

"Where are we going?" she asked, taking the gun from his hand, and holding it in her own. She checked to make sure it was safe to put away before placing it back in the glove compartment. There was no way she was traveling with that thing at her back.

"First stop is the casino. I get the rundown of what I've got to do, and then we'll go and check it out."

"Sure, okay, I can handle that." She rubbed her sweaty palms down her thighs.

You can do this, Lou.

"You're a unique woman."

"I don't think you mean that as a compliment."

"I do. You're memorable."

"I like how you're not trying to pretend to be someone you're not."

He chuckled. "I'm not going to pretend that I've not fucked other women. You've been with other men. What matters now is what we do with each other."

She noticed her gripped the steering wheel tightly. "What do you mean?"

"This is a date. I'm not going to be seeing other women. I'm not going to be fucking anyone else but you."

"I've not said I'd fuck you."

"You will. It's inevitable."

"Are you really that good?"

"I'm the best."

"Wow, you really have an ego, don't you?"

"It's one I've earned, baby."

Glancing out of the window, it was only seven, and the sun was slowly setting in the sky. She rolled down the window to allow some air into the car. It was damn hot, and if she'd been at home, she wouldn't have even bothered getting dressed.

They passed a rough part of the city, and she saw women of all ages on the street corners already looking for customers for the night.

"You're sad, why?" he asked.

"Do you deal with women like this?" She looked over at him. "Women on the streets?"

He sighed. "We deal with women, Lou. It's the oldest trade in the world. We don't deal with these on the streets, and if I see a pimp mistreating his woman, then I step in."

"Do you deal with women? Hurt them if they stop earning enough?"

"Fuck! No, I don't. We have men who deal with that shit. We do go to the brothels to make sure everything is good. None of us accept men abusing the women."

Lou snorted. "Right? You're just straight up guys."

"We'll make one of the stops tonight, and you'll get to see the other side of it. Some of these women, they come to us to earn a living, not the other way around."

"You don't kidnap women? Force them?"

"Fuck, no! There's enough women who want to do what they do. We don't have to fucking force them."

"Women actually want to do this?"

"It's easy money. Fucking always is, and we have more than enough clients who like to pay."

"What kind of clients?" she asked.

"The kind who don't want their shit known to the world."

"You're having a lot of faith in me tonight."

"Yeah, well, I'm also putting you at risk."

"What do you mean?"

"If you tell anyone of what you see tonight, you won't live for long enough afterward."

"You'd kill me?" She figured as much.

"Got no choice. I'm putting a lot of trust in you as well."

"Why?"

"Consider it a hunch."

He didn't go into detail, and she didn't press him.

Chapter Six

Jacob had done his research on Louisa Moore, and had come to the conclusion that he wouldn't hold anything back. Lou wasn't the kind of woman who was thrilled by diamonds and luxury. She liked to get down and dirty. The jobs she'd taken had proven that. He'd even heard she'd been a waitress for a short time, a cleaner after that. Each job showed hard work, and it made him wonder if she was trying to make up for her parents' complete lack of care.

Riley wasn't all that helpful. He spent most of his time avoiding questions about his sister. Fortunately, there was always a paper and internet trail with everyone.

Pulling into the parking lot of the large casino, Jacob ignored the frenzy outside, and rounded the car to help Lou out of the car.

"Welcome to Dentons'."

"Out of all of the names you could think of?"

"What can I say? We just love our name."

She giggled, and he loved the sound. Taking hold of her hand, they entered the large casino. The sound of the slot machines, the music, and the squeals of success filled his senses. Moving toward the elevator, he saw Bruce, his mother's guard, at the door.

"Where's my mother?" he asked.

"With your father, and so I don't get in the way, I stay here watching. Who is this?"

"This is Louisa Moore. She's with me."

Bruce pressed a button, and the elevator opened.

Stepping inside, he placed his hand at Lou's waist, and they entered. Bruce stepped inside with them.

"Riley's fight was fantastic," Bruce said.

"Thank you."

"You should be proud of him."

"Yes, I am."

She didn't sound it, and he stroked her stomach moving up just slightly so that he could graze the underside of her breast. She took a deep breath, and he smiled, wondering if she wanted to kick his ass. Staring at their reflections in the shiny metal, he saw her nipples were tight and pressed against her shirt.

Bruce was paid to be silent, and not to notice anything. Jacob had fucked women with Bruce being present. He was a damn good bodyguard, and loyal as fuck.

The elevator stopped, and the doors opened.

"You know the way."

Jacob keeping his hand at her waist, they made their way down a long corridor toward his father's main office. Knocking once, he waited for Maddox's call to enter. He didn't have to wait long. Entering the room, he saw his brothers Abel and Gideon were there already. His mother and one of his uncles were also in the office.

"Hello, Jacob," Charlotte said, coming toward him. She cupped his cheek, kissing him on either side, before moving toward Louisa. "We haven't been introduced."

"Mom, this is Louisa. Louisa, this is my mom, but everyone calls her Charlotte."

"Apart from my kids that is. It's a pleasure to meet you, Louisa."

"It's Lou. Nearly everyone calls me Lou." He watched as she shook hands with Charlotte. His mother wasn't about to let that happen, and pulled Lou in for a hug.

"He's brought you up here. That must mean something."

"Charlotte, step back," Maddox said, getting out of his seat, and leaning in front of his desk.

Jacob had already clocked the gun, and he was so damn angry as he stared at his father.

"This is not necessary. She's a Moore," Charlotte said.

"It needs to be done." Maddox stared at Lou as his mother moved away. "You know what we do, right?"

"I have an idea."

Jacob didn't care what his father said. He wasn't going to leave his woman's side.

Maddox placed the small pistol in his lap, his finger on the trigger ready. Slowly, Jacob moved behind his back, and pulled out the second Glock he kept there. He nudged Lou and placed the gun within her hand.

His father respected women who could stand up for themselves.

"I don't agree with Jacob taking you out tonight. What you see, what you hear, you don't. If I so much as hear a whisper that you talked to anyone, I will kill you." Maddox raised his gun and pointed it at her. Jacob tapped her waist, and Lou pointed her own gun at him. Maddox looked surprised, and Jacob only saw it by the slight twitch by his mouth.

"I understand. I don't like having a gun pointed at me, Mr. Denton. I find it very uncomfortable."

"You wouldn't even think of firing it."

A scream filled the space as Lou moved, and a bullet was fired. Jacob held her tightly, and Maddox looked down at his desk.

"You missed."

"I didn't miss. I was aiming for that spot. I can shoot you if you want."

"You know how to work a gun."

Jacob was so damn hot right now. His cock pressed against the front of his pants wanting inside her.

"My brother doesn't believe a woman should be

made vulnerable. The city is a dangerous place for a woman. He trained me, and I'm a pretty good shot. Want to see?"

"Fuck no." Maddox laughed. "I like her. She's got some spunk inside her."

Charlotte moved toward his father and took the gun out of his hands. "Is that any way to treat a future daughter-in-law?"

"Wait? What? I'm not—this is not that. It's just a simple date."

"No man brings a woman to the family business for a simple date, Lou." Maddox clapped his hands. "Anyway, let's get down to business."

Lou handed Jacob the gun, and he put the safety in place, putting it in the back of his pants.

Jacob stayed put with Lou by his side as his father started to talk.

"I've been hearing some troubling news out of our red zone," Maddox said.

Jacob tensed up. The red zone was what his father said about their escorts, their brothels.

"What news?" Abel asked.

"I got a call today that they're taking girls off the street. Young girls, underage girls, and forcing them. You know I don't like that shit. I want it shut down, and dealt with."

"I'll do it," Jacob said.

"Good. You've got a call to Frank as well. He's near that district."

During the meeting Maddox told them what he needed, giving them all certain jobs, and when it was over, they all relaxed.

Releasing Lou, Jacob stepped up to his father's desk. "Who gave you a call?" he asked.

"One of our women. She said it has gone bad.

I've not been able to send anyone out there for a few months, and it looks like they think they can do whatever the fuck they want, and I will just leave it. It's about time that they see I'm not a man to be fucked with."

Nodding, Jacob turned back, going to Lou. "Are you sure you're ready for this?"

"Yes. With what he said about the red zone, is that, erm, the brothels?"

He nodded. "Yes. Dad doesn't agree with forcing women. We're heading over to give them a surprise visit. You're going to see some stuff you're not going to like."

They made their way toward the elevator. Abel held the door open for them.

"Damn, Lou, you're fucking hot. I've never seen a woman hold a gun to my dad, but shit, I'd pay to get my rocks off."

"Back off," Jacob said.

"Whatever. It's true then? The possession?"

"Yes."

He didn't want her to know what he was talking about.

"Damn, you're pussy-whipped."

"Fuck off!"

The elevator opened up. "Stay safe, brothers," Jacob said.

"Same to you. Keep checking in," Gideon said.

They left the casino and were in the car within seconds.

"Wow, you don't exactly linger with each other."

"We have work to do. We don't have time to stay around, chatting or shit. There're family events for that." He helped her into the car, rounding the vehicle to climb in beside her.

"He mentioned Frank's, where I work?"

"Yep. It's owned by the Dentons."

"Great. I've been working for you all along."

"Do you feel like giving the boss some perks?"

"Nope." She chuckled. It was the first real humor he'd heard from her, and he liked it. He wanted to keep on hearing it.

"Buckle up."

Turning over the engine, he pulled away from the casino, and was on his way to the red zone.

"You know, according to the movies and books, most families like yours are into human trafficking."

"Again, it's something that makes us different. Dad couldn't do it. If the woman wants to sell her shit for him, then he'll help, keep her safe, and make sure she has a good life. We don't believe in forcing."

"You know that does sound crazy, right?"

"It doesn't. Dad couldn't do it. He'd see women and put Mom's and Tamsin's faces to them. It would kill him, and that's not what we're about."

"So, have you killed people?" she asked. "We're allowed to ask questions."

"Yes, I've killed people."

"Women?"

Jacob gripped his steering wheel tightly. "Yes. I had no choice. She was in pain, and she begged me to end it for her. I did." It wasn't one of his fondest memories, but it was one he'd come to accept.

"An act of mercy?"

"Yes. She'd been beaten to a bloody pulp, and she was completely broken. I ended her pain. I later found out that if I hadn't have killed her, she'd have died anyway. Her body had already started to shut down."

"You're really a contradiction, aren't you? The whole family. No one can put you into one box and tick bad, can they?"

Jacob shrugged. "It's not my job to make

everyone's life easier. We do what we do. Am I saying we're good people? No, I'm not. I'm saying we do what needs to be done."

"Killing people?"

It was tempting to let her know that Riley had ended lives with his hands for his parents. He decided against it. Jacob had no intention of coming between brother and sister. The last thing he wanted to do was start their relationship in a bad place.

"Like I said, I wouldn't say we're good people. We're just better than some, and worse than others." Jacob shrugged. "I deal with it. Now, it's time for me to ask a question."

"Okay, hit me with it."

"Have you ever shot a person?"

He glanced over at her and saw her cheeks were bright red. "You have?"

"It was an accident. I shot Riley in the leg while he was training me. It was a complete mistake, and I took him to the hospital. He wouldn't talk to me for so long. For a time I thought he'd never talk to me. He did though."

Even though Lou had a fuck off attitude, he saw that she was a good woman, a kind one. Tamsin had been calling him asking if she was going to be stopping by the house any time soon. His sister was a good judge of character, and she liked Lou.

"I can see Riley not talking to you, maybe even having a pet lip."

"He did. It stuck out like right out here." She smiled. "It took me three months of ice-cream making, cooking his favorite foods, and sitting with him watching old movies before he'd forgive me. There was also some begging, and groveling. A lot of groveling."

Jacob liked this. He liked talking with her, and he

loved the sound of her voice.

I'm fucking pussy-whipped and I've not even gotten the chance to screw her yet.

Once again he was left gripping the steering wheel while his dick throbbed against the front of his pants. Just another night of struggling through with a hard-on for him.

****

The rooms were dark when they entered the brothel, and it did look like something on one of those seedy films that she'd seen. Lou stayed beside Jacob as he walked down the long hallway. There hadn't been anyone to greet them on the door, and that had pissed him off.

"What's the matter?" she asked.

"Someone should be on the door. How the fuck are they supposed to monitor the men who come in if they're not fucking there?" He snapped each word out, and his body was tense.

Keeping silent, she followed him down the long corridor until they came to a door. Moans, groans, and the occasional cry filled the air.

Heat filled her cheeks as she imagined what was going on behind closed doors.

"Don't say anything. Do as I ask, and don't argue."

"Got it."

Jacob opened the door, and she noticed he held onto the gun at the base of his back but didn't make a move to pull it free.

Glancing into the room, Lou's stomach rolled. There were drugs, sex, and alcohol all around. The room was covered in filth, used condoms, and she was sure some men hadn't even tried to clean away their cum stains. It was gross, and nothing like what Jacob had described in the car. This was exactly what she had imagined, and it didn't disappoint even if it did turn her stomach.

"What the fuck am I seeing?" Jacob asked.

The room froze, and Lou watched as a man pushed a woman off his cock, and got to his feet. "Mr. Denton, I didn't know you were coming."

"No, yet as far as I'm concerned it shouldn't matter when I turn up or not. We have a standard. Where is the guard on the door? Why the fuck are there drugs? And why, David, have I heard that you've stolen women off the fucking streets?" Jacob stormed up to the man, grabbing him by the lapels of his stained jacket.

Lou grabbed the gun behind her back and waited until she would need to use it. She changed her attention from looking at Jacob to around the room. He had a gun pressed to David's throat.

"I want fucking answers now."

Several men had their hands held up.

"Lou," Jacob said.

"Yeah?"

"Call Maddox, tell him we've got a serious problem with David and the red zone, and I need some backup."

She caught the phone that he threw her way, and found Maddox's number. She relayed the message and waited.

"He says to hold down the fort. He'll have backup to you in ten."

"Take care of him, Lou. Is it bad?"

"Yeah. This is just, wow, it's awful, Mr. Denton."

"Maddox. You're working with Jacob. You get to call me by name." He hung up, and she stared down at the blank screen.

Charming man.

"I want you all to separate. Women, over there, men, over there," Jacob said. "You, stay the fuck there." He pushed David into a seat and stepped back. "Where is everyone?"

"The bitches are working," David said. "We're doing good for business."

"You call this good? I call this a fucking shithole. This is not what we handed to you, David. We gave you the rules, and now we've got rumors of people stealing women. Not good." Jacob kicked over a table that had lines of coke and straws. "This is not what we're about." He walked over to a woman that looked completely fucked. Her eyes were glazed over, and drool was coming out of her mouth. Jacob grabbed her face. "What's your name?"

Slurring ensued, and Jacob let her go. She dropped to the floor and passed out.

"This is fucking disgusting. The women undergo health checks. They're not allowed to take drugs, and so far, it looks like you're breaking those rules. We offer them a life, a chance to make their way in the world."

"They're fucking whores!" David spat the words out.

Jacob grabbed a wooden chair and threw it at David, who then collapsed on the floor, screaming in pain. "They're not fucking whores. You treat them with respect. They're damn good workers, and we promised them respect. You're fucking with our name with this shit."

With each second that passed, Jacob clearly got angrier.

Lou stayed silent, watching the man at work. He looked terrifying.

"Who are you?" he asked, grabbing a man's cheeks.

The guy mumbled something, and Jacob sighed. He looked totally disgusted.

"What did I miss?" Abel asked, coming up behind her. "What the fuck!"

Okay, she had no reason to doubt Jacob with the way Abel was reacting. Clearly, this was not how the brothel was supposed to be.

Lou left them alone, and curiosity got the better of her. Growing up, she'd always been told that her curious mind would get her in trouble. But no matter what, it never stopped her. She found a door going through to a kitchen. There were no one around, but then she heard a faint cry. Frowning, she moved a little closer into the kitchen, and the cry became a sob, and louder.

She found another door partially opened. "What the hell is with this place and doors?" Slowly, she opened the door a little wider.

"Please, stop, I just want my mommy. Please, ouch, it hurts."

The cry tore at Lou's heart, and without thinking, she stormed down the basement stairs. There was a young girl, dressed in a school uniform, who was screaming and crying to be released. A man, twice the girl's size was trying to force his dick inside her, but the girl was wriggling. The man had a belt in his hand and was whipping her.

"I told you, cunt, you're going to give me what I fucking want." He brought the belt down on her, and the young girl kept on screaming for her mother.

Every protective instinct within Lou came alive, and she charged at the man, grabbing the leather of the belt in her hand, and tightening her fist even as it hurt more than she could have ever imagined. She didn't have a clear shot of the man as both were moving, and Lou's hand was shaking.

"Stay away from her." She fought the pain in her hand.

The man turned, slamming his fist against her face, and Lou collided with the wall, screaming out in pain.

"Look, an older bitch. I'll deal with you later."

The gun dug into her back, and she watched the man slap the girl. Reaching for the gun, she quickly pulled the safety off, and aimed at the man's leg. It was the only way she knew she wouldn't hurt the girl as well. She fired the bullet. He immediately went down, and the girl screamed.

Getting to her feet, she urged for the girl to come to her, which she did.

Lou heard the men running toward her, and she held the gun shakily in her hand, pointing it at the man. The girl had her arms wrapped around her, and was so scared her body shook with fear.

"What the fuck?" Jacob asked.

"He was attacking this little girl. She just wanted to go home to her mom." Loud held the girl tightly.

"Fuck! I'm going to kill those fucking bastards."

"No one is going to hurt you," Lou said, trying her hardest to comfort the young girl.

Jacob came forward, asking her name.

"Sh, it's okay. He's one of the good guys. He's my friend."

"He was hurting me. I was just walking home, and they snatched me. Told me I was a whore and all whores had a place in the world."

"I've already put a call into Luke," Abel said.

"Who is Luke?"

"He's a cop we know on the force. He'll get her home, make sure she's safe. I've also talked to Dad. He's going with Luke and Mom to make sure she's taken care of. They're pissed, Jacob. I don't think this is going to be opening for some time," Abel said.

"They broke every single rule." They made their way out of the basement, and Lou did her hardest not to show that she was in any kind of pain. Waiting in the main hallway she was surprised that they didn't have to wait long. Maddox, Charlotte, and an officer in uniform came through the door.

Lou handed the girl over and stepped away. Her face hurt, as did her side. She hurt all over.

"What the fuck did that bastard do to you?" Jacob asked, taking hold of her chin, and turning her head this way and that.

"It's nothing."

"Fuck if that isn't nothing."

She took his hand. "He hit me, that's all. Do we have to stay or can we move on?"

Jacob looked over her shoulder toward his father.

"Go. We've got this. This needs us to clean it up. I've already contacted my brothers. They'll be here to help me."

Jacob took her hand, leading her away from the brothel.

"I take it tonight is a really bad night?"

"It's the worst fucking night. Everything I told you we weren't was completely fucking twisted inside that bastard place."

"You sound pissed."

"I am." Jacob started up the car, and Lou turned toward him, watching.

"Where are we going now?" she asked.

"I'm heading over to Frank's."

Lou reached for the visor and flipped it down, seeing the bruise already forming on her cheek.

"That bastard will pay for what he did to you."

"It's no big deal. I shot him."

"I'll handle him."

"When?"

"My father knows to keep him safe for when I've finished tonight."

"We're not going to dinner?"

"We are, but you see, a Denton never finishes work."

Ten minutes later they walked into Frank's strip club, and she was pushed at the bar. Seconds later, Riley was there, and he was cupping her face.

"What the fuck happened?"

There was a lot of *what the fucks* going on. "We found a bad guy who had no problem hitting girls or women." She cupped her cheek and winced.

"Will you keep an eye on her while I talk with Frank?" Jacob asked.

"Sure. She's my sister. Of course I'd take care of her."

Ben handed her a shot of whiskey, and she took it graciously, throwing it to the back of her throat, and swallowing it down. She needed the burn.

"Are you going to tell me what happened?"

Lou gave him a rundown of what went down.

"I'm going to kill the prick who touched you."

"Calm down, Riley. I shot him in the leg. This is—it's dangerous work what you're going to do with Jacob. Please, promise me you won't do anything stupid," she said.

"Lou, this is me."

"Exactly, it's why I'm asking."

"I'm not going to do anything stupid. I promise." He wrapped his arms around her, and she winced. Her side was hurting.

Jacob chose that moment to come out. "I need to

borrow your office, Frank," he said. Without asking for her consent, he grabbed her hand, and pulled her into the small space of Frank's office.

"Have you done your business?" she asked.

"Remove your shirt."

"What?"

"You hurt when Riley hugged your side. Remove it. I want to see."

"It's nothing."

"It was enough to make you wince."

Annoyed, she pulled the shirt over her head. She wore a white vest, with a crop top underneath.

Jacob took over, gripping the edge of her shirt, and lifting it over her head. She froze. The bra she wore wasn't padded. The room grew just that little bit smaller. Jacob pulled the crop top over her head, and she heard it fall to the floor. Staring into his dark brown eyes, Lou couldn't look away. He held her captive.

She tensed up as his fingers touched her side, sliding up.

"Does it hurt?" he asked.

Forcing herself to look away, she stared down at his large, masculine fingers stroking up her side.

"No, it doesn't. The guy, he pushed me, and I hit the wall. Just a few bruises maybe." She looked at him and took a step back. Jacob moved closer to her, and the air seemed to thicken between them. He was taller than she was, making it so she had to tilt her head back to see him.

She took a deep breath as his thumb grazed the underside of her breast. Her nipple puckered, and she tensed up. For some strange reason, she wasn't afraid of him.

He moved his thumb up, and traced back and forth over her nipple. Lou didn't try to stop him.

"I'm not easy," she said.

"I know." Jacob moved his finger over the lace of her bra, and tugged it down so that her breast spilled out. He leaned in close, pressing his lips to hers. His gaze stayed on hers, and then he took her nipple between his lips, sucking it into his mouth.

Heat flooded her pussy, and she cried out as his teeth bit into the bud. He soothed it out with his tongue. She pressed her legs together to try to ease the need that had started.

Someone knocked on the door, bringing their time to an end.

"I think it's time we go to dinner."

****

Later that night, Jacob entered the basement of the red zone district. His father and mother were still there, as were his uncles. While he'd been with Frank, he'd put the call through to make sure the fucker who was shot in the leg was still alive and breathing when he got back.

The rest of the night had gone by without a hitch. He'd taken Lou with him on several runs, scooping up cash, and keeping an eye on basic business. All the while, her bruise had gotten deeper, covering her cheek.

Riley was pissed at him.

He didn't need her twin to be pissed at him. Jacob was already pissed at himself. No one hurt his woman.

"Where is he?" he asked.

Maddox moved aside from the basement, and he walked down. Abel sat in a seat in the corner. The two men, David the manager they had put in charge, and the one who hurt Lou, were sitting in the middle chained to each other.

"I'm sorry, man, I thought I was doing a good thing."

"A good thing? I checked the books, David. You've been scamming off these women for months," Abel said.

"You touched my woman," Jacob said, pointing at the man he didn't know.

"Look, every bitch in here wants to be touched."

Slamming his fist against the man's face, Jacob thought about Lou, her smile, her face, now with a bruise. He'd been so busy dealing with David that he'd not been there to protect her while she'd been protecting an underage girl. Over and over he slammed his fist, alternating between his hands, landing against the man's face. Jacob didn't stop. He kept on hitting him.

Only when he'd had enough of hitting did he go for the bat that Abel was holding. This was another element that made the Dentons different. They were all more than happy to take care of business.

He didn't stop, tuning out the man's scream as he thought about Lou. No man was ever going to lay a hand on her, he'd make damn sure of that.

Chapter Seven

"Lou's gone back to work," Riley said, climbing into the car Friday evening. He carried two cups of coffee and placed them both in the cup holders. They had already had one night together, and Jacob was impressed by him. His father had done well picking Riley out of a lot of applications.

"What?"

"Lou's back at work. She wouldn't listen to me even though half of her face is black and fucking blue. Fucking woman, I tell you she just can't stop. She's always had to be doing something, as otherwise she goes crazy."

Riley was dressed in an expensive suit, but Jacob didn't accept anything less. "I told her that I spoke to Frank."

"Exactly, and she spoke to him that she wanted her shift back. Staying in her apartment baking oatmeal cookies isn't going to keep her going for long."

"Lou bakes?"

"Yep, she has for a long time. It was something she learned when we were young. Mom and Dad employed a cook, and Lou would spend all hours in the kitchen with her. They got close, and then because our parents are fucking evil, they fired her ass, leaving Lou heartbroken about it for weeks afterward."

"Speaking of your parents, we've got to pay them a visit."

"What about?"

Jacob paused. He didn't know if it would be a good idea to tell Riley his father's suspicions. Landon had been approached in high school about doing more fights, and they believed it was the Moores who'd done it.

"Come on, just spill. I know you're going to be wanting to have more than a date with my sister. Whatever else you've got about our family, just hit me with it. I know that our family isn't the most liked."

"Most liked?"

"Yeah, we've got older brothers that are petty criminals that just piss everyone else off. My parents are hungry for power and money. They find out that you've got a thing for Lou, and they would be all over it. They're gaining enemies every single day."

"How are you and Lou not affected by your parents?"

"You mean, why are we so different?" Riley asked.

"Yeah."

"By the time Lou and I came along, they'd already been dealing with the fights. They weren't around all that much. We got nannies, cooks, staff to take care of us. They're awful people, shit parents, but they knew how to pick a decent nanny. Put simply, Jacob, we weren't raised by our parents."

It made a lot of sense to Jacob. "You can tell."

"I know our parents, and even our brothers aren't liked. We're used to it."

"How does Lou handle your fighting?"

"She doesn't, not really. We're brother and sister, twins, but to be honest, we're really great friends as well. I know, clichéd as shit, but it's the way it is with us," Riley said.

"You taught her how to shoot, and that came in handy."

"Yeah, she comes across as this hard ass, but she's really not. I wanted her to be able to protect herself."

Jacob liked Riley, he really did, which was a

change for him. Usually he could only stomach his brothers, which was why his guards that his father put on his ass stayed far away. Jacob wasn't known for playing friendly, and he doubted that he would ever be.

They were silent for several minutes, and Jacob took a drink of the coffee.

"So, what happens with the red zone? David is no more, and I heard the brothels have been closed since Wednesday. That's got to be a shitload of dough wasted," Riley said.

"It's not. Maddox is interviewing potential candidates. If he could, he'd put Bruce inside them, and be done with it."

"Bruce? He the guy guarding your mother?"

"Yep, and Dad's not about to let him leave my mother. He loves her too damn much."

"Speaking of love, how does this whole, 'Lou is mine' thing work? Do you just know? Is it a feeling? I don't want you to fuck her over."

Jacob glanced over, not understanding why he was suddenly so chatty. "What the hell is going on with you?"

"I'm bored, and I figured I may as well check out the guy who wants to be with my baby sister. In case you didn't know, she's only a couple of minutes younger than me." Riley grabbed his coffee, taking a sip. "Lou, she loves with her whole heart."

"How do you know that?" he asked.

"I've known my sister since birth. You've known her just over a week. Give me a break, I know my fucking sister okay? She talks the talk, but it's all a cover. She's sweet, and I tell you what, she'd make one heck of a mom. We were out shopping about a year ago. I wanted to buy something for the woman I was seeing, and I didn't have a clue what to get her. We're in the mall, and it's busy, I mean fucking no space kind of busy. It was insane, and I just wanted to leave. On the way out of the store, there's this little kid. A girl, and she stood there at the door with her thumb in her mouth, couldn't be more than three. I don't remember what she was wearing, or even what she looked like other than the fact she was young. Lou, she crouched down so the girl wasn't afraid, and started talking to her." Riley chuckled, but it was more of a disgusted sound than anything else. "People were coming and going, and even though I was moaning, Lou wouldn't be rushed. She waited until the girl took her hand, and together, they started to hunt every single store to find her mother. For over an hour, Lou was searching for the kid's mother. Finally, the mother came rushing toward us, sobbing, and hugging her kid. Lou could have simply handed the brat over to security. She didn't. Once you have Lou's love, there's no backing out. She's all in, and that is never going to change."

Jacob liked that. She had a sweet heart.

"I won't hurt her."

"You better not, otherwise I'm going to kick your ass."

For the rest of the night they made their way around three strip clubs, checking over the books, and making sure the business was running smoothly. Maddox had his own reasons for doing things the way he did it. He could just hire a bunch of men to report the business dealings within each venture, but Maddox didn't trust anyone but his sons. It's what made the Dentons so damn powerful. No one could predict their next move. They were all over the place, and Jacob was damn thankful for that. He'd never survive in a nine-to-five job, nor could he ever stomach being kept in a box with a computer.

Once they were done, Jacob headed toward

Frank's strip club. He'd have gladly gone straight to the club, but he needed to deal with his responsibilities first.

"You just can't go a long time without seeing her, can you?" Riley asked, chuckling. "I like you."

"Riley, we work together, and you're Lou's brother, but I will put a bullet in you if you even think to start with all that shit, do you get me?"

"Get you? I get you. Can't help but laugh. It's so fucking funny."

Jacob parked the car, and together they headed into the busy strip club. It was the only club in the ten mile radius that was actually doing really well. He knew his father was considering cutting several of the clubs to recoup some money, putting the women in other places.

Buttoning his jacket, he took a seat at the bar, while Riley collapsed into another one beside him.

Jacob had already seen Lou. She was near the stage, watching one of the strippers perform.

Glancing up at the stage, he saw it was Pam, one of the women he'd screwed a long time ago.

"That's not going to do well for you, is it?" Ben asked.

"I'm not going to be keeping any secrets from her. I'm going to tell her the truth."

Riley laughed. "I wonder if she'd still be friends with Pam afterward."

"She doesn't have to worry about anyone." Jacob didn't have eyes for any other woman.

"You got any problems with me taking Pam out for a test drive?" Riley asked.

"Go ahead. She's not mine."

"You're not even jealous?"

"Nope."

"You whipped, Jacob?" Ben asked.

He glared at the barman, and then at his woman's

brother, letting them both know not to mess with him. Jacob watched as Lou made her way toward the bar. She was staring at him, looking somewhat nervous. He'd not seen her since their night together where she'd shot one of the men in the red zone.

"Hey guys," she said. She glanced over at Riley and winced. "Are you here to, you know?" She gave a little whistle, which only made all the men fall all over themselves laughing.

"It's not funny."

"It is, sis. You should see yourself. Yes, I'm here to fuck one of your many friends." Riley got up from his seat. "How do you think I feel knowing you're fucking my boss?"

"I'm not." Lou's cheeks heated, and Jacob chuckled. "Don't even start, you!"

He grabbed her hand, tugging her close. "There's something I want to ask you." Getting to his feet, he nodded toward Ben and Frank as he came out of the back room. Jacob didn't care what anyone thought as he walked into one of the private rooms. He wasn't an idiot. He knew what went on inside them as he'd taken a few women back here a time or two before he met Lou.

"Jacob, I'm not comfortable—"

He cut her off, pressing a finger against her lips. "I'm not expecting to fuck you, babe. I just want to talk, and I know this is private."

Taking a seat, he pulled her so that she was straddling his waist.

"This is very presumptuous of you, Mr. Denton."

Grabbing her ass, he squeezed the plump flesh. "I like you in my arms, babe."

"You're calling me babe a lot. What's up?"

"Every Sunday my mom does an entire lavish dinner. I want to take you as my plus one."

"You're inviting me to dinner?" she asked.

"I am." He squeezed her ass, and she moaned. Jacob moved his hand down, curving around to cup her pussy. She tensed up, and he simply kept his hand still. "I'm not going to hurt you."

"You're touching me."

"You're not fighting me."

"This is not fair."

Leaning close to her, he pressed a kiss to her lips. "I'm a Denton. I don't play fair."

"Dinner?"

"Yes. If it makes you feel any better, Riley will be there. It's something my dad likes to do. Invite his new employees so he can get a feel for them."

"Will he be getting a feel for me?"

"No. You're there because I want you to be there."

"This is a lot more than a night out working."

"You didn't work with me."

She chuckled. "You're not going to back down, are you?"

"Would you really want me to?" Jacob wasn't going to stop. She belonged to him no matter what she said.

"I don't know."

"Well, when you do, let me know." Moving his hands up her back, he sank his fingers into her hair, pulling her in for a kiss. "Let me taste those sweet lips."

****

"What are you doing?" Riley asked.

Lou wrapped up the plate of brownies that she had made. She'd made several plates of brownies as she didn't want to go empty handed. "I've never been to dinner before. What does a person do?"

Her brother shrugged. "I don't know. Eat, drink,

compliment the cook."

"Ugh, this is insane. I don't have a clue what I'm doing. I should have told him no."

"You were in one of the private rooms for a long time. Do you have anything you want to tell me?"

"Stop it."

"I think you're being a bitch, making him work that hard for it."

"You're supposed to be my brother. You know, support me in the fact I don't sleep with the first man who looks my way."

Riley sighed, walking toward her and taking a brownie from the top of the pile of the third tray she'd baked. "Lou, I know what you did when we were younger. You don't think I've been worried about you. Our parents, they're awful people. Jacob—he's not like our parents. He's a good person, and I think you need to give him a chance."

"You've been working with him for a couple of days, and you're telling me to give him a chance?"

"Exactly. You should do what I say. I know what I'm doing." He winked at her to which she rolled her eyes. She loved her brother, but there were times he didn't take things seriously.

"I'll do what I think is best for me."

"Good. While you're doing that, I'm going to keep on nagging you. You're my sister. I want you happy."

"I am happy."

"Lou, honey, you spent most of your life trying to piss off our parents. It's not exactly happiness."

She shrugged. What he said wasn't a lie. Most of her adult life had been about pissing her parents off. Lou refused to do a single thing that they said. They drove her crazy with their constant interference. They only wanted her to further their own agenda.

Slapping his hand, she finished wrapping the brownies just as someone knocked on her door. She figured it was Jacob, and she let Riley answer the door.

Jacob entered her apartment, and she watched him, shocked by the change in his appearance. There was no sign of the suits he liked to wear. He wore blue jeans and a black shirt. He looked good, damn good.

Licking her suddenly dry lips, she did her best to smile at him, and not show her sudden attraction to him.

"You baked?" Jacob asked.

"Yeah. Is it okay? It's only brownies." She nibbled her lips now as her nerves got the better of her.

"She's so nervous," Riley said. "She's never been invited to dinner."

Jacob chuckled. "You've got nothing to be nervous about."

"Well, there's more than enough brownies here to last them a few days." When she got nervous, she baked. It was a stress reliever for her.

"They're going to love it."

"They're good," Riley said, taking a bite of the one that he held in his hand.

"I'll save it until after dinner." Jacob kept on looking at her, and there was something intense in his look. Lou didn't know what it was, but it made her anxious.

No, it didn't. The look he was giving her went straight to her pussy, and she wanted him badly.

"Right, I'm going to go and wait in the car." Riley left her apartment, and she stared at Jacob.

"How have you been?" she asked.

She hadn't seen him since he came to invite her to his parents' place for dinner. Yes, it had only been a Saturday, but still, she had watched the door waiting for him to visit her.

What is wrong with you?

He's not your guy.

Lou didn't even know what they had with each other. Were they a couple? Were they dating? She was confused by what they were doing.

Jacob stepped up close until he was in front of her. He cupped her face, stroking her cheek. "I've missed looking at you."

"You saw me the other night." Her heart fluttered. No man had ever looked at her the way that Jacob was. He looked like he wanted to devour her. He ran his thumb across her bottom lip, and he sighed.

Before she could say anything, he claimed her lips, pressing her up against the counter in the kitchen. He moved one of his hands to her waist as his other cupped her cheek. Jacob slid his tongue across her lips, and she moaned.

"Open for me, babe," he said.

She couldn't deny him anything, so she opened her lips and gave him access. His tongue plundered her mouth, and she couldn't help but moan. Jacob didn't stop. He took possession of her mouth as if it was his right. Jacob held her like she belonged to him, and instead of being angered by it, she fucking loved it. Wrapping her arms around his neck, she gave herself over to the pleasure of his mouth, his touch, everything.

He rocked his cock against her, and she gasped at the prominent bulge of his cock.

"I want to fuck you," he said.

Right then, right there, she didn't have any objection to him taking her.

She gripped hold of his shoulders, pulling away, to stare into his dark eyes.

"You'd let me right now, wouldn't you?"

Nodding her head, she stared at his chest, trying to compose herself.

"Are you wet for me, right now?" he asked.

Lou returned her attention back to him and cupped his cock. "And you're rock hard for me right now, right?" She squeezed his dick, almost offering him a challenge.

"Baby, you're playing with the wrong man. I'm the fucking master of this game." He didn't just cup her pussy. He pushed his hand down her denim skirt, inside her parties, and touched her. She tensed up, pressing her thighs together, trying to hide her obvious arousal from him. He wouldn't let her, so he pushed a finger between the lips of her pussy, stroking over her clit. "You're soaking wet."

"Stop."

"Your lips are telling me to stop, but your pussy is begging for me to continue. What's it going to be, Lou?"

"Riley is wait—"

"He'll wait. Do you want me to stop?"

She shook her head.

"Not good enough, Lou. I need to hear the words from your own lips. Shaking your head is not going to cut it."

"Please," she said. "Don't make me."

"Don't make you beg?"

She nodded. Why were words evading her? Lou couldn't recall a time in her life when she'd not said what she wanted. Jacob, he made her forget herself. He surrounded her, and she liked it.

"For me to take you, you're going to have to beg." He pulled his hand out of her pants and sucked his fingers. "It's time for us to go to dinner."

He picked up two trays of brownies and headed

toward the door.

"That's it? Is this what it's about? You want to tease me just to show me you can have anyone."

"I've never said anything like that to you."

"What's this about then?" she asked. "Are you just having fun? I know about Pam. She told me all about you." Lou watched him tense.

"You've spoken to Pam?"

"She saw us coming out of the private rooms, and told me not to even think of falling for you. You're not the kind of guy who gives himself. You're a fuck them and leave them kind of person. Is that what you're wanting? To fuck me?"

I shouldn't care.

Lou did. She did care so damn much it hurt.

Jacob moved toward her, placing the trays back on the counter. "Don't listen to anyone else. Yes, I fucked Pam, and I walked away. She was nothing more than a willing pussy for me to use for the night. I've fucked a great many women, and I'm not going to pretend I haven't. There have been a lot of women."

"And what? I'm special?"

"You don't even have a clue how special you are to me." He captured her chin, holding her in place. "It's okay. I can wait until you see what's going to happen between us. We're going to fuck, and it's going to be so good you're going to think of nothing but my cock inside you, and I'm going to give it to you every single way I can. Until then, don't be jealous. You're the only woman who has made it to my parents' place. Yes, you are special." Once again he kissed her lips, and she didn't want his kiss to end. He broke away, grabbing the brownies. "Let's go."

Chapter Eight

Abel had brought a date with him, and they were all grilling him. Jacob was surprised as they never took women, or their easy fucks, to their parents' house for dinner. Lou was with his mother as he'd introduced the two when he first entered. The brownies had been taken straight to the kitchen to keep them out of his hands.

"Is she the one?" Gideon asked.

"Nah, there's no way she's the one. She looked like a schoolteacher," Landon said.

"What the fuck is the problem? I brought a woman. Why does there have to be anything?" Abel asked.

"You do know that our parents believe we'll only bring 'the one' back home?" Jacob asked.

"Like you? How is your dating going with Lou?"

"It's not," Riley said, butting into the conversation.

"We didn't ask you," Jacob said, glaring at his partner, and future brother-in-law.

"You didn't, your brothers did. So how does this work? Do you just see a woman, and that's it? You're in love, and you can't have any other woman?" Riley asked, looking at all of the brothers.

Jacob glanced at his five other brothers. His sister was nowhere to be seen. She was probably hiding out in her bedroom. She wanted to join the parties, yet she was the shiest one of the bunch.

"I don't know. You'd have to ask the guy who's been caught." Damian spoke up, turning to look at him.

All of his brothers' eyes looked at him.

"You're in love with my sister?"

Jacob sighed. "I don't know how to describe it. It was like I turned, and she was there, and everything just seemed to stop. All I could focus on was her. All I wanted was her." He remembered the moment he saw her, the way his world just seemed to open up.

"Yeah, but Lou's not exactly giving you the easiest time of it, is she?"

"It's not a two way thing?" Abel asked.

"No. I spoke to Mom because I assumed it was, but it wasn't. I feel everything, and yet she feels nothing."

"It's not all bad, boys," Charlotte said.

They all turned to their mother. She held a tray of drinks, and he took a glass of water. With all of them driving, his mother wouldn't allow them to drink alcohol.

"You didn't love Dad straight away?" Landon asked.

She shook her head. "It took me time. I'm sorry, boys. You've been given a legacy of falling for one woman, and having the work that you do, but you've also got to make the woman fall for you." She patted Jacob's arm. "I have every faith that you'll make it work. Louisa is a wonderful girl."

"She's not letting you call her Lou?" Riley asked.

"Oh, she is. I just like her full name. It's nice, and beautiful." Their mother left, and Jacob released another sigh. He'd never had to work hard to get a woman. Like the strip club that Lou worked at, all he had to do was point at the woman he wanted for the night, and she'd come to him on her knees if he wanted her to.

"How are you making her fall for you?" Landon asked.

"Why? You wanting to get some tips?"

Landon's face went beet red.

"Oh, has Landon found himself a girl?" This came from Oliver.

"Fuck off. All of us are supposed to fall hard like

Dad. What's wrong with getting a few pointers from our big brother?" Landon asked.

"Lou's not like every other woman. We can't share pointers about this, guys. This is going to be different for all of us. What I want to know is if the schoolteacher is Abel's woman?" Jacob asked, putting the pressure on Abel.

"She's not a schoolteacher, and she works at the casino at several of the tables. I like her. She's nice."

"Nice?" Gideon asked.

"Yeah, nice."

Gideon turned to him. "Is that how you see Lou? She's nice?"

"No. It's not what I see when I look at my woman."

"Okay, fine, she's not *the one,* but I like her. She's nice, and she's a good girl, hard worker."

Jacob shook his head. "You've got to be careful. If she's not the one but she's a nice girl, you're going to break her heart when you find the right one."

Abel shook his head. "You ever thought that the supposed legacy is not going to hit all of us?"

Their father interrupted them by laughing. "You boys, you really don't get it, do you?" Maddox asked.

"What? What don't we get?" Landon asked.

"You're *all* going to find your woman. I agree with Jacob about this, Abel. I told all of you boys that you would find a woman for yourself, a woman you're not going to be able to walk away from. Once you find her, and you will, the woman you're with, she's going to end up hurt. It's not going to be something you can control. It's just the way it works."

"How do you know?" Abel asked.

"I watched my brother go through it." Maddox pointed toward Stuart, his youngest brother, and their uncle. "He married the girl he dated in school. He was in love with her, and they had a child together. By twenty-seven years old, he was married with two kids, and then he met her."

Jacob looked toward the corner where Michelle stood.

"Michelle caused quite a stir when Stuart first met her. He didn't want to hurt his wife, but she wasn't the one. It's difficult for them all, and Michelle feels like she ruined a family even though she did nothing wrong. All she did was answer an ad."

Michelle had gone for a job as a nanny. On the first meeting, Stuart had been torn.

"Be careful. Don't become the bastard that Stuart has to live with. He has to watch his kids grow up with another man, and Michelle has to deal with the kids not being happy with her. It's a fucked up situation," Maddox said.

Their father left them alone, and Jacob wasn't in the mood to talk anymore. Leaving his brothers to keep pestering Abel, he moved toward the entrance in the kitchen. Lou's hair was now bound up in a ponytail, and she was kneading some bread with his mother beside her.

He'd never expected to enjoy watching his woman in the kitchen with his mother, but seeing Lou, it did something to him. This was what it meant to have a woman of his own, and being able to bring her home.

Lou looked up, her gaze landing on his, and she smiled. "Hey," she said.

"Ah, Jacob, come on, show Lou that you know a thing or two within the kitchen."

Entering the kitchen, he removed his jacket, and moved beside Lou to start kneading another batch of bread. His mother was one hell of a cook, and she loved to make several loaves of bread to give to her sons for when they left.

He loved her bread. He loved all of her food. If he didn't work out three times a week, he'd have developed a serious problem. Jacob did love good food.

Standing beside Lou, he grabbed the bowl that had the risen dough. Removing the plastic wrap, he punched it down and gathered it out onto the floured counter.

"Well, well, well, I didn't know you even knew what a kitchen was." Lou bumped him with her hip, and he chuckled.

It was the first time she actually looked relaxed in his company.

"This is excellent work. Lou, you're a darling." His mother moved to the stove and started stirring a large pot. "I've been making plenty of leftovers for you to take home. You know I don't like the thought of you guys living on fast food."

"Fast food is a curse to everyone," Lou said.

He kneaded the bread, standing closer to her.

"Do you like to cook?" she asked.

"Not so much. I used to enjoy helping Mom in the kitchen."

"The boys were never allowed in the kitchen until their father was satisfied with their training."

"Yeah, everyone gets to train but me. I'm expected to be in the kitchen all the time," Tamsin said, jumping up onto a stool.

"Stop that pouting, honey. You're not going to be training like your brothers," Charlotte said.

"I know because I'm a girl," she said, wrinkling her nose. "Lou, do you think it's fair?"

"What? Sorry?"

"Tamsin," Jacob said, trying to warn her not to draw his woman into the conversation.

"What? I'm only asking?"

"I love being in the kitchen," Lou said. "I've never been one for the whole fighting thing. That's Riley's job."

"What's it like being a twin?" Tamsin asked, resting her chin on her hand.

"How do you mean?"

"Do you feel Riley? Know when he's hurt? I watched this documentary once that said twins are connected or something like that."

"How old are you?"

"Ten, why?"

"It's just you talk a little older is all."

"Around here, you have to in order to be heard," Tamsin said.

"Oh, don't start with that nonsense," Charlotte said, moving up behind her daughter. "You're heard all right. You're just too damn spoiled."

Tamsin stuck her tongue out, which made Lou laugh.

"Don't encourage her," Jacob said.

Lou looked at him beneath her lashes, and his cock throbbed, remembering what it was like to have her in his arms. He was nowhere near winning over her heart, but he knew how to make it so she was begging for him.

****

The Dentons' dinner was not what Lou was expecting. She sat opposite Jacob with her brother beside her. The table was large, and conversation was about everything and nothing. She'd half expected work to be a big topic of conversation, but it didn't even enter a single conversation. Movies, books, school, football, and even the news had all been discussed.

"You never did tell me," Tamsin said, drawing

her attention once again. The young girl was sitting between Jacob and Landon.

"Tell you what?"

"Do you and Riley share a special connection?" Tamsin asked.

The table went a little silent.

"Connection?" Riley asked.

"With us being twins, she wants to know if we feel each other's pain, or something like that," she said, explaining to her brother.

"You're asking me if we're weird?" Riley said, smirking.

Tamsin shook her head. "I didn't mean any disrespect."

"It's not something I talk about all that much, sweetie. It's not as simple as knowing she's in pain, but I get a feeling. We shared space for nine months, you know. She's my little sister." Riley pulled her in for a hug.

"He fell out of a tree house once," she said, recalling the moment even though she had been in her room studying at the time. "I didn't know where he was, but he broke his leg, and I remember so strangely, touching my leg as I felt a twinge, maybe just an itch. What freaked me out was when we got to the hospital, it was where his leg had broken. Creepy."

"We can't feel each other's slaps or anything like that. It's more of a gut feeling that something is wrong, and in a serious case like her leg, there's a pain," Riley said.

"What about pleasure?" Jacob asked.

Lou turned to the man who had her all over the place. Heat filled her cheeks. "What?"

"Pleasure, can you feel it?"

"Jacob, please, that's private," Charlotte said.

"No, I can't, thank God, that would just be fucking creepy." Everyone laughed at Riley's words.

The rest of the meal went by without a hitch, and even though they all said they couldn't eat another thing, Lou watched her brownies disappear.

"Damn, those are so good."

At the end of the night, Riley got a lift off of Abel, and holding some food for herself, she climbed into the car.

Lou couldn't get the memory of them together out of her mind. He'd touched her, and all dinner she'd tried not to think of what it would be like to be with him. There hadn't been a single guy she had enjoyed sex with, and yet she wanted it with Jacob.

"It was a nice dinner," she said.

"Yes, it was. I'm glad you enjoyed it."

"Your mother is one hell of a cook."

"I'm sorry about Tamsin. She gets nervous at family gatherings like that. When I told her you were coming, and so was Riley, she started looking at everything to do with twins."

Lou chuckled. "She's a nice girl. A little firecracker. She's going to have the boys running rings around each other. I hope you can all handle that."

"She's not my problem. I'm just the big brother."

"She loves you though. I saw that." It reminded her of the love she had for Riley. He was her true family. Part of her was envious of the way the Dentons were with each other. It was a loving family.

A fun loving crime family.

Forget about that.

"You and Riley, you're really close?"

"Yeah. I've told you before. It's just me and him for a long time."

"Do your parents know about us?"

"No. I avoid talking to them." If her parents knew Jacob was sniffing around her they wouldn't leave her alone about having him as a potential husband. She hated her parents. They only did what was good for themselves.

"What are you doing next week?" Jacob asked.

"Erm, I'm working Monday through Friday. I've got the weekend off." She tucked some hair behind her ear.

He reached over taking hold of her hand, locking their fingers. She stared down at their joined hands, noticing his slightly darker skin.

"Have you been on a vacation?" she asked.

"Not recently."

Lou nibbled her lip wondering what the hell to say. For the past couple of days Jacob had been the one to do all of the talking. Now, she was finding it hard to say something to him or to draw him into conversation.

Before long, he was parking up outside of her apartment, and she stared up at the tall building.

"Do you want to come up?" she asked.

"Sure. I could do with a coffee."

It's just coffee. Nothing is going to happen. It's just coffee.

Even as she kept assuring herself that nothing was going to happen, she couldn't help but hope that something did happen. She wanted him, and there was no denying it. Her pussy was damp, and she wanted to continue where they left off.

They made their way up together, and she was aware of the heat of his hand at her back. Her mouth went dry, and all she wanted to do was wrap her arms around his body, getting him to take her.

You don't want him to take you.

You want him to fuck you, to make it hurt, and

then soothe out the pain.

She pulled her keys out of her pocket, and even as her hand shook, she entered her small apartment.

Jacob closed the door.

The air was thick with tension.

Entering the kitchen, she filled the kettle and placed it on to boil. Jacob came up behind her. Both of his hands rested on the counter, trapping her against his hard body so she had nowhere to go.

His mouth brushed across her ear.

"Do you want me, Lou?"

Her pussy grew wet, and she hated it.

"Are you used to everyone falling for you?"

"I'm not interested in what everyone else wants." One of his hands left the counter, and he touched her stomach. She sucked in a breath, but Jacob didn't stop there. He moved his hand up to cup her breast. "I'm interested in knowing what you want." He pinched her nipple. "You don't want to be attracted to me, do you, Lou? You want to fight what this body wants but you're turned on by me, and that pisses you off."

"Jacob?"

"I'm not a good man, Lou. I've killed people, and I've done it without caring. It's easy to me. I've been trained to kill. It's what I do." He nuzzled her neck at the same time he teased her nipple, soothing out the pinch. "You see, baby, I'm a patient man. I'm not used to working for it, but I don't mind waiting for you. I'm not going anywhere. I won't have that coffee after all. I have a long day." He pulled away, and she watched as he placed a cell phone beside her. "I've programmed all the numbers that you need. Use it."

"I've got a phone."

"Not as good as this one. I'll be seeing you, baby." He spun her around, dropping a kiss to her lips.

"Think about me."

She watched him move toward the door, closing it behind him.

Lou touched her lips, then flicked the locks into place before turning off the kettle. She was not interested in drinking right now. The dinner with his family had gone into late evening, and it was a little after eight.

After taking a quick shower, she sat in front of the television, holding the cell phone that he'd given her.

She clicked the buttons going into the contacts, and found Jacob's number. His brothers, her brother, and even his parents were all there.

Lou: **This is my new number.**

Staring at the television screen she didn't know what was actually playing when her cell phone beeped.

Riley: **I know. You accepted his gift?**

Lou: **I didn't have a choice.**

Riley: **Stop being a bitch and give him a chance.**

She smiled but didn't respond. Lou had been determined to keep Jacob at arm's length, but he was more determined to keep her in his life.

Lou hovered over his name, wondering if she should send him a message. He was a hard man to forget. Pam had told her not to get her hopes up, but then the other woman hadn't looked pleased when she told her that Jacob was pursuing her.

Pam was normally a nice woman but just recently she had shown her true colors, and Lou would watch her back around her.

Lou: **Thank you for the phone. I like it. X**

She sent the message then cringed. What if the kiss on the end was too much?

Jacob: **You're very welcome. XX**

Lou chuckled and rolled her eyes. He wouldn't let

her have anything.

Chapter Nine

Three months later

Jacob stood in the basement of the casino watching as Abel worked over the snitch who had tried to cop a deal with some attorney. Their father was working with their own attorney to have the evidence disappear, and while that was happening, they were going to make sure everyone knew not to fuck with them.

"I'm sorry, I'm sorry, I'm sorry," the snitch said, whimpering.

"You're sorry now?" Abel slammed his fist against the man's face, and a tooth got thrown across the room.

"You're driving my sister nuts," Riley said, coming to stand with him, and handing him a folder.

Jacob smiled thinking about the past three months. It had been a long time since he'd gotten any pussy, but the only pussy he wanted was that of Riley's sister. "What about her?" Jacob had listened to his mother, taking her advice. For the past three months, he'd been dating Lou, taking her out on long dinners, walks, the movies. He'd even gone to museums and art exhibits. He texted her constantly, and he'd done everything with her apart from have sex.

Jacob figured with Lou he had to catch her a lot differently than other women.

"I'm doing no such thing."

"Please, I know Lou, and you're confusing the fuck out of her. I have to say, I like your style." Riley slapped him on the back.

Flicking open the folder, he was reading up on the snitch who was currently learning a lesson about backing out of deals.

Jacob whistled. "You've got two wives, and six children. Fuck me, you've been a busy guy."

"Please, don't hurt them," snitch said.

"How were you going to look after them?" Jacob asked, moving to stand in front of him. Abel left the snitch alone as Jacob started to question him.

"I don't know."

"Our sources say he was going to get a new identity. Hide away so no one could find him," Gideon said.

"Hiding from your wives and kids. Do they know about each other?" Riley asked.

"Please," the snitch said.

"Yep, they know now. Both women are finding out who he married first to see who is going to need that divorce. Look at this, they both want alimony." Jacob whistled. "Snitch on us, new identity, and both women get nothing."

Snitch dropped his head. There was blood everywhere, but Jacob didn't care. Closing the file, he handed it back to Riley. He gripped the man's hair and pulled his head back. "Now, how did you find out about the underground fights?"

"Everyone knows about it."

"The video you got. Where did it come from?"

"I don't know, man. I just picked it up."

Jacob shook his head. "Who are you protecting?"

"I'm not protecting anyone." The man started crying. "I just needed a way out. I took the picture. I went to one of the fights, and I filmed it."

"It was of Landon," Maddox said, entering the room followed by his uncle Stuart. "The fight with Landon and Riley where no videos were allowed." Maddox held the cell phone.

"You got it?"

"It seems the attorney he went to has a gambling problem. I got the film before he reported it to his bosses, and his debt disappeared and a hundred grand was deposited into his account," Maddox said, turning to Riley. "Your identity is secured."

"Thank you, sir."

Not only would they have had to deal with shit because of the fight, but because of Landon being a minor, it would have hit the family hard, then Riley would have also gone down. It would have been a royal shit-storm.

Lou wanted him to keep her brother safe. She asked him to promise. One promise and he had no intention of breaking it.

"I told you, Riley, I appreciate what you did. Landon's been told to stay out of trouble until it all blows over," Maddox said. Jacob placed a chair in front of the snitch, and watched his father take a seat. "Two wives, huh, Harold? I always said your dick would get you in trouble. You should have come to me."

The snitch, now known as Harold, started sobbing.

"You know I have issues with leaving kids without a father. You've completely tied my fucking hands." Maddox sighed. "I could kill you right here, right now, and that will be the end of it. Your two families will leave in peace, or I take a kid from each marriage, how about that? Trade you for two?"

Jacob was disgusted as he watched Harold think about it.

His father didn't hesitate. He brought his gun up and fired a bullet. "No man puts his kids in his place. We'll clean this up," Maddox said, taking the file from Riley. "Go on to the red zone again. I want to make sure that house stays up and running."

After they had found the young women and even the girls from the red zone being taken from the streets, they had used their cop informant to help them take the girls home. Maddox wanted the zone constantly checked to make sure no one else was going to try something stupid.

Climbing into the car, he waited for Riley to do his seatbelt before heading in the direction of the red zone.

"As a brother, I thought you'd be happy that I'm treating Lou like a princess."

"I am, but I'm thinking she needs a little more," Riley said. "All she does is ask about you. Is that your way of getting under her skin, to make it so she's always thinking about you?"

His little scheme had been working. During his dates with her, he made a point of touching, stroking, getting to know what turned her on and what didn't. Lou was a very receptive woman, and he'd made sure to tease her at every opportunity. When they stayed in, he picked highly erotic movies, and while the sex was playing, he made sure to caress her body.

She never outright begged for him to fuck her, but her body always looked ready. Her eyes spoke a great deal as well. He loved watching her fight her own need.

"Most brothers would do their hardest to keep their sister safe."

"Pfft, I know that Lou is safest with you. I've seen the way you look at her, and the way you stop other men looking at her."

"I don't know what you mean."

"Okay, you want to go there. That first night at Frank's, you nearly killed that businessman. A couple of months ago, one cowboy paying a visit to the city had touched her ass. You followed him into the bathroom, and when he came out, he was sporting broken fingers and a black eye."

"He walked into the door and trapped his fingers."

"Yet you didn't hear a thing."

"Lou didn't want her ass touched."

"You protect her. She wants something, and you give it to her. The only thing you've not given her is a puppy, and I know for a fact, you tried to sweet talk the owner of the apartment building, but it has something to do with health and safety as to why they can't have pets or something. Believe me, Jacob, you're the best damn guy around. Your brothers are the same. All of the Dentons are protective, and I doubt that's ever going to change."

"You're giving me your brother seal of approval?"

"Yep, I am."

Jacob parked up a few yards from the red zone entrance, and he was pleased to see a guard on the front door.

"Hello, Mr. Denton, Mr. Moore."

They entered the building, and Jacob was more than impressed with what he saw.

"You can't interfere with Lou and me," he said.

"I've got no plans to. I've told you. It's between you and Lou. I want her happy, and this time, I'm going to do what I think is best for my sister, and that's you."

****

Lou popped her gum and waited for Ben to finish up the tray. She was still working at Frank's, and she had no intention of quitting the job. News had gotten to her parents that she'd been seen out with Jacob Denton, and so far she'd been able to avoid him.

"Hello, sugar," Frank said, taking a seat beside

her.

"Just doing my job."

Frank was a sweet man, and he didn't seem to mind Jacob coming around to see her even when he tried to keep boyfriends out of his strip club. Ben was a boyfriend, but he also wasn't jealous of his woman stripping.

"Your parents were here Sunday night."

She had every alternate Sunday off. The strip club was open every single day apart from Christmas Day. "Did they cause any trouble?"

"I called Riley, and he came and dealt with them. They were asking questions about you and Jacob."

Wrinkling her nose, she glanced toward the door. "I'm really sorry. I can't believe they keep coming here." They had a couple of fights tonight so she'd miss them, she hoped.

"Don't let them get to you."

"I sometimes think I should just not have anything to do with Jacob." Even saying the words made her uncomfortable. She liked Jacob, which was a shock to her. Lou had never expected to like Jacob, and now the best part of her day was seeing him. He always made a point of either seeing her before work, during, or taking her home. If he couldn't make it at any of those times, he visited her apartment.

Still, no sex.

She really wanted to pout about that.

Jacob would touch her, but he wouldn't go too far, not since that first day she went to dinner with his parents. They had gone to several Sunday dinners, and she had grown close to the whole family. Tamsin was sweet, and the young girl called her regularly as well.

"Don't ever think or say shit like that," Frank said. "Your parents are not worth sacrificing your happiness just so they can get what they want."

"You're a sweet guy, Frank."

"Honey, if Jacob hadn't claimed you, I had every intention of doing the deed myself. I know a keeper when I see one."

She wrapped an arm around her boss and gave him a hug, not believing him.

"Get your hands off my woman," Jacob said.

Lou slowly removed her hand, and turned to see the man who wouldn't sleep with her.

You've gone from refusing to sleep with him, to now all you want to do is fuck him.

He was driving her crazy, refusing to do anything more than touch.

"Don't start being a caveman." She looked past Jacob and didn't see her brother. "Where's Riley?"

He'd promised her that he would keep Riley safe, and she trusted him to.

"Riley went home early. I came to wait for you to finish."

"Go on home early, Lou. You've earned it," Frank said.

"Are you sure?"

"I'm giving you the rest of the night off. Don't make me forget it." It was her weekend off, and she gave Frank a big smile. "I'll grab my bag."

She grabbed her bag and made her way back out to the main bar when she saw Pam sitting between Frank and Jacob. Lou paused as jealousy struck her hard.

Staring at Jacob, she saw that his hands were in his pockets, and he was glaring at Pam.

Moving toward his side, she linked her arm with his. Pam liked to constantly talk about the amazing sex that they had shared.

"Hello, Lou, I didn't see you there. I was offering

Jacob a show."

"Did you want a show, baby?" she asked, looking up at Jacob. "I'm sure I'd love to see you give a private show."

"You know I only want you. Goodnight, Frank." Before she could say anything more he pulled her away from Pam out toward his car. "What the hell was that?"

"Did you want a private show?"

"No."

"Why not? It's not like you're getting any from me, is it? You must be getting it elsewhere. Pam's told me how damn determined you are to get what you want, and I know without a doubt you're not getting any here." She pointed at her own body. "You must be getting it somewhere." Her voice had risen to yelling, and she didn't even care who heard her.

"Is that what this is about, Lou? You don't like the fact that I've taken my time with you? You want me to fuck you, is that it?"

"Are you screwing Pam?"

"No."

He opened his car door and pushed her into the car. She slammed her palm against the window, annoyed with him. Jacob got behind the wheel, not saying a word as he pulled away from the strip club.

Lou folded her arms, and she refused to be the one to speak. This was not her problem.

When he drove away from her apartment, Lou frowned. "You've missed my turning," she said.

He didn't stop, nor did he answer, but he kept on driving.

"What is going on, Jacob?"

Once again, he didn't bother talking to her, and he kept on driving. Her heart raced, and she looked outside the window at the passing scenery. Twenty minutes later, they pulled up to a gate, and Jacob rolled his window down.

Her heart began to pound as he pressed his card to the scan, punching in the number that opened the gate. Wherever they were going was secluded.

He started driving straight, and she looked behind her to see the gates closing.

"Jacob, what's going on?"

No words were spoken, and she gritted her teeth.

Minutes passed, and he pulled up outside a luxury house.

"My father gave this to me on the night of my eighteenth birthday. He believes every man has a right to have a home. All of his sons, and Tamsin, will have a home to call their own." He climbed out of the car, and she grabbed her bag, doing the same. Jacob grabbed her hand, and pulled her into the house.

The door closed, and he had her pressed up against the hard wood door.

"I've not been fucking anything other than my fist, thinking about you the entire time." He grabbed her bag from her hands, throwing it across the entrance hall. Jacob gripped the edge of her shirt, and tore it from her neck down. She released a little squeal as he took her by surprise with his brute force.

He pulled away long enough to remove his jacket, being careful to place it on the coat hook beside the door. Next, he unbuttoned his shirt, and her mouth ran dry. His hard muscles were covered in ink, intricate designs of flowers, graves, and patterns that didn't seem to link together, and yet did on him.

"Do you really think there's any way I'd want anyone else when I've got you to come home to?"

Jacob grabbed her hand, locking them together, and placing them above her head, so she was stretched tall with her back against the wall.

He tore the shirt completely from her body so she was standing in her white lace bra.

"Fuck, baby, I've been thinking about these tits, you've been driving me crazy with the memory of them. I love how deep red they are, and big, waiting for me." He tugged the lace of her bra down, and he leaned in close taking one bud into his mouth.

Lou's eyes closed as he sucked her nipple into his mouth. There was no way she could control her body's response to his touch. She wanted Jacob, and he held her in place as he sucked her nipple. He circled the nipple, then used his teeth to create that spark of pain before lavishing his tongue back and forth.

An answering fire started to build between her thighs. Her clit filled, getting bigger, and she wanted to touch herself. She had never had such strong feelings before, but with Jacob, he'd been building a fire within her, and he was finally going to light the torch.

She wanted to go up in flames, craving it more than she had ever craved anything else in her life.

He held her tight against the door, and she couldn't do anything as he pulled away. She released a little whimper, and he chuckled. "What's the matter, baby? You want me to fuck you? Is that why you had your little outburst?"

"Why?"

"Why what?"

"Why have you waited?" she asked. Her voice was husky as she struggled with her own needs taking over.

"I've fucked Pam. I've fucked a lot of women in my time. I told you I didn't live like a monk. I've never lied to you."

"Why have I been different?"

Jacob sighed. "Those women were easy. They were easy holes to fill. You're not easy, baby. I never thought you were."

"What make me different?"

"You belong to me. That's what makes you different. You're mine."

Chapter Ten

Jacob slammed his lips down on hers, changing his hands so that he could use his other to pull the lace of her bra back, exposing her perfect tits. They were large, and he wanted them over him bouncing as he fucked her hard. His cock pressed against his pants, and he wanted inside her so damn bad. He'd bet his fortune that she was dripping wet, and wanting his cock.

He'd give it to her as well—when he was ready.

She screamed his name as he took her other breast between his teeth, biting down just a little and then soothing it out with his tongue. Lou arched against him, pressing toward him, yet trying to get away. He kept her locked in place, letting her know without a doubt that he was the one who controlled her. The only way she was getting away from him was if he allowed her to.

Once they crossed this line there was no going back. He wasn't going to let her get away, and he also wasn't going to give her a warning. Releasing her hands, he grabbed her jeans, pulling them down her thighs, waiting for her to step out of them. He waited for her to be on two feet before he lifted one, and she jumped twice finding her balance. Bunching her panties in his fist, he tore them from her body, and stared at her pussy. The lips of her sex were bare, no trace of pubic hair.

"You wax?" he asked.

"Yes. Regularly, I don't like anything down there." Her voice was husky, and her chest was flushed red. Nodding toward the light switch, he ordered her to flick it on.

The entrance hall lit up, and he got a good look at his woman. Her size eighteen curves drove him wild. She had thick hips and thighs, the kind that made a man want to be between them all the time. Her tits were nice and big, hanging down, swaying a little. She held onto the wall, and her lips were moist.

Returning his attention to her pretty cunt, he saw her lips were coated with her cream, and he wanted a taste of her pussy.

They were in his home, and now she was stuck with his rules. He wasn't going to ask for permission in these four walls. He was going to take what he wanted, and right now, he wanted to lick her creamy pussy.

As he swiped his tongue across her slit, the musky taste of her exploded on his tongue. She cried out, and he ran his fingers up the inside of her thigh, stroking the entrance of her cunt. Sliding two fingers within her, he pulled away to watch her body suck him inside. Her pussy was tight, and it sucked him up, knowing what it wanted.

"Lou, if you wanted me to fuck you, all you had to do was ask."

She whimpered, and he chuckled, pumping into her as he sucked her clit into his mouth.

"Oh, God, that feels so good." She rubbed her pussy on his face, thrusting her hips in time to him pumping his fingers inside her. He added a third finger feeling how wet she got as he pumped into her. She was fucking begging for it.

He loved being around Lou. She was a sweet woman, a vulnerable and caring woman, but she tried her hardest to hide it. This woman was not sweet. She wanted to be fucked, and desperately.

Pulling his fingers out of her pussy, he moved them back to her ass. She tensed up, and he rubbed her cream against her puckered hole. Pressing a finger inside her ass, he heard her wince, and he'd only applied a little pressure.

Flicking her clit a final time, he pulled his fingers

away, wiping them on his pants, not caring as they smeared in a streak on the leg. Lou lowered her leg and stared at him. He pulled his belt off, letting it drop to the floor. Next, his jeans fell, and he wrapped his fingers around the length of his cock.

"Look at me, Lou."

Her gaze dropped to his cock, and he watched as she visibly swallowed.

The tip leaked pre-cum, and he started to massage it into his length. "You ever had a cock in your ass?"

"No."

"You ever had a man as big as me?"

"No."

The smart ass had gone, and Jacob truly believed he got to see the real Lou. Stepping forward, he released his own cock, and wrapped an arm around her. Pulling her out of the entrance hall, he made his way down toward the sitting room, turning on lights as he went.

"Do you have staff?"

"They're gone at night," Jacob said. He wouldn't risk anyone seeing his woman naked. Lou was all for him. At the sitting room, he turned the light on, and placed her on the edge of the seat. She lowered back, and he spread her thighs wide, staring down at her pretty, naked pussy. "You surprised me with this, Lou," he said, running his fingers down the plump flesh of her lips. They were still slick, and he'd not let her come. The taste of her was still in his mouth. "Have you ever gotten dirty?" he asked.

"Dirty?"

"Sex, Lou."

"I don't think so."

Plunging two fingers inside her, he watched her cry out, her eyes closing. Pulling them out, he held them up, rubbing his thumb against the slick digits. "I don't do fucking proper, nor making love. I like it to be real, no holding back, baby."

She swallowed once again, and he couldn't wait to see her swallow his load as he pumped it into her mouth. "I've never done that."

"You're in for an awakening tonight." Gripping his cock, he rested his length between the lips of her sex, and he slowly pumped backward and forward. He bumped her clit, and she moaned out his name. "That's it, Lou. I want to hear my name screamed from those lips."

She tried to thrust up against him, but he wouldn't let her. Grabbing her hips, he held her in place, staring down at his swollen cock with the tip leaking pre-cum. He left a trail across her clit, and it smeared up, covering a little more of those plump lips.

"Please, Jacob."

"Please, what?"

"Fuck me."

"What do you want me to do?" he asked.

"I want you to fuck me."

"Do you want my dick inside you?"

She nodded. "Yes, please."

"Tell me, baby." Moving his hands down to her pussy, he spread the lips of her cunt, and pushed his cock over her clit. Each movement had her gasping out his name.

"Put your cock inside me, please, please," she said.

He pulled away from her and paused at her entrance. Staring into her eyes, he slowly eased inside her, taking his time, relishing the first thrust within her tight cunt.

Lou gripped the edge of the chair as he thrust inside her, an inch at a time.

Jacob wasn't a small man. Several women had complained about how big he was, and when he slammed the last inch within Lou, she gasped out, arching up. He felt her cunt tightening around him, clenching his cock hard.

"Fuck me, baby, you feel so damn tight."

He stared down at where they were joined. Her pussy lips open slightly, touching the fine hairs around the base of his cock. They were one. His cock was deep within her, and he wasn't going anywhere.

Running his hands up her body, he flicked the catch of her bra, pulling it off her.

She threw the bra across the room, and he started to pull out of her. His cock was slick with her juice.

"Jacob!" She screamed his name as he slammed every inch back inside her. This time he didn't give her a chance to grow accustomed to him. He fucked her hard, pounding the length of his dick deep inside, opening her up with his rough claiming. Her tits bounced, and he cupped her ass, needing to come. When he felt that he was close to spilling his cum inside her, he pulled out, sinking to his knees, and capturing her clit between his teeth. Using his fingers, he fucked them inside her, flicking her clit, tonguing her.

She was so soft, and dripping with her arousal.

The time they had spent together had heightened her need. Jacob had been taking care of himself each night with his hand, and he was curious now as to how Lou had been taking care of her own needs. Had she waited?

He'd ask her as soon as he was done eating her out. Filling her cunt with three fingers, he went as deep as he could, trying to stretch her. Tomorrow, when she was walking, she was going to remember who had been fucking her.

"Jacob," she said, crying out his name, and a second later, she came all over his fingers. He pulled out of her once again, stroking over her clit, and then filled her tight pussy with his cock as she was in mid orgasm. He groaned out as her pussy tightened around him. It was the best feeling in the world, and he pounded his dick deep inside her. He kept stroking her pussy until she was thrown into a second orgasm, and then a third. All the time, he fucked her hard.

When she came a fourth time, he moved his hand away, and wrapped his arms around her, holding her tightly as he pumped his spunk inside her, filling her up. Even though he'd been beating off regularly, he believed that he'd filled her with enough spunk to run a small sperm factory.

Claiming his lips, he plunged his tongue within her mouth.

The pleasure ebbed away, and he stared into her green eyes.

Her cheeks were flushed as she stared back at him.

"I've not fucked Pam or any other woman since the night I met you. The same night Landon won the fight."

"You haven't?"

"I've not been with Pam for a long time, Lou. She's just trying to make you jealous. There's nothing between us. There never was. Don't let jealousy get in the way."

She touched his cheek, running her thumb across his lip. "What have you done to me?"

He smiled. "I could say the same to you."

"I didn't care, Jacob. The men before you, they didn't mean anything. You, it's different, and that scares me."

"I'm not a good man."

"No, you're not." Tears filled her eyes, and he wiped them away.

"I'm not a good man, Lou, but with you, I'd be the best damn man there is. No one will be better than me." It was what his father was to his mother.

They were monsters, and yet, their women were the most cherished.

"My parents?"

"I'll handle your parents. This is not about you chasing me. I know that, and you should know that. This is something different, something more."

He was in love with her. It wasn't just the legacy either. Lou had gotten under his skin, and in the last few months he'd fallen for her as well. He loved listening to her laugh, being with her, and sharing everything.

"This home, it's yours, Lou."

She gasped, glancing around. "No, it is not. That's crazy, Jacob."

"Didn't you hear? The Denton men are all crazy."

Lou chuckled. "I doubt that. There's no way an entire family is crazy." She chuckled, and then groaned as his cock started to swell.

"Be careful. It has been a long time since it has been inside a pussy."

"You're being dirty."

"With how wet you are, I'd say you fucking loved it." He eased out of her and stared down just in time to see his seed spilling out of her. "Time for a bath I think."

****

Jacob was completely different with her as he carried her upstairs into his bathroom. He placed her on the toilet, filled a monster tub, and then urged her into the water. Lou sighed as the warm water surrounded her.

You've just had sex with Jacob freaking Denton.

She watched as he climbed into the tub in front of her. It was surreal to her as she stared at him. He was a handsome man, sexy, and she understood why people like Pam wanted to make her jealous. Jacob was the kind of man who didn't go with women like her. Lou wasn't a model, never would be, but she'd always been happy in her own skin.

Her pussy throbbed, and she drew her knees up against her chest.

Jacob reached out, gripping her knees, and spreading her legs open. He didn't stop there. He moved close, stroking his hands down to grab her hips. She loved his touch, and every second that she spent with him, she found she liked him even more. He wasn't the man she thought he was. Jacob was so much more.

Lou squealed as he hauled her over him, getting her to straddle his thighs. The action was so unexpected that she gripped his shoulders.

He chuckled.

"You're not very funny." She smiled though.

"I wasn't trying to be funny."

She wrapped her legs around his waist, and then her arms around his neck. "I feel like I have to pinch myself."

"Why's that, babe?"

"You, and this, and everything. If someone had told me four months ago I'd be straddling *the Jacob Denton* after dating him for several months, I'd have laughed at them." She teased the hair at the back of his neck, liking how familiar she was with him. "Surreal."

He stroked her back as he pressed a kiss to her chest. His cock pulsed against her pussy, and she glanced down to see that his cock was thickening where it rested between their bodies.

"You're ready to go again?" Not that she had a complaint.

"I've got a healthy appetite." He tucked some hair behind her ear, and she stared into his eyes.

Jacob held her captive. For three months, he'd wormed his way into her heart by his constant persistence. Yes, he was a bad man, and he did bad things, but with her, he treated her like she was the most treasured thing in the world.

"Why me?"

"You're going all serious on me?"

She chuckled, looking down at his stomach. Licking her lips, she tried to get under control. Her emotions were all over the place. He'd been driving her crazy with need, and now that she'd had sex, she was scared. Lou hadn't wanted to be with Jacob, and now, he was part of her, and she'd given in to her own need. This was more though. Biting her lip she was afraid to ask, but she had no choice.

"Have you had your fun? Did you get what you wanted?" This wasn't her being a bitch. Old insecurities started to flood her being, and she couldn't hold them back.

He cupped her chin forcing her to look at him. "What the fuck is that?"

"Well, you've got what you want, right? You can move onto the next woman." She really didn't want him to.

His jaw clenched. "You think I'm that fucking fickle?"

"What? No, of course not." She didn't know what to expect from him. Pam had been feeding her horrible tales about Jacob, and she shouldn't have listened to them.

His anger shook her to the core.

"Lou, fuck, if all I wanted was a fuck I would have screwed you the night I took you to my parents' for dinner."

"You're presumptuous."

"And you're being fucking stupid if you think for a second that you wouldn't have given it to me. Don't be a fucking bitch on me now. I got that you were in the beginning because you didn't know me. You know me now, so don't be something you're not. The bitch, she's for the outside world, not between us. I've been here with you, Lou. Every single time I've touched you, you've fucking wanted it. There's not been a moment when you haven't." He dropped his hand into the tub with water splashing over the side of the bath.

Tears filled her eyes as she saw the hurt look. He was right. She had just been the world's biggest bitch, and Lou regretted her actions. She was fucking stupid.

"You don't get it, baby. You're it for me. This is far more than getting a fucking screw. You've seen the bitches that have tried to give me their number, the way they are. If I wanted to fuck, I could have phoned them." He cupped her cheek. "I'm not that man. This is it for me. You've got to believe me."

"I'm so sorry. I shouldn't have doubted you, and I won't do it."

He shook his head.

"No, Jacob. I am sorry. I owe you an apology, I just—this kind of stuff, it doesn't happen to me, okay. I listened to Pam—"

"That was your first mistake. Don't listen to bitches that don't get what they want. Pam, she wanted more. I'm not giving her it, and now she's after you. Be the better woman, Lou."

"I'm sorry."

"Good, now prove it to me."

Jacob sank his fingers into her hair, pulling her in close so that his breath fanned across her lips. He slid his tongue against her lip, and she opened up, moaning as he plundered her mouth. She sank her own fingers into his hair, holding him tightly to her. This was more than just sex, and hearing him say that eased her troubled mind.

After years of only ever doing something to piss her parents off, Lou was finally doing something *she* wanted.

"You're moving in here," he said, pulling away from the kiss.

"What?"

"This place, you're moving in with me. I've taken you now, claimed you, you're not going anywhere else. You're the one I'm coming home to every single night."

She snorted. "Don't you think you should ask?"

He shook his head. "Nope, you'd only argue with me, and find some smart assed comeback. You're mine, and it's time you realized who you belonged to."

Before she could comment, he lifted her up, moved his cock, and slowly lowered her over him.

All argument fled her brain as her body awakened with his dick sliding to the hilt within her.

"Oh, fuck, baby. You're so tight and perfect." He stroked her back, caressing down to grip her ass. Jacob tightened his hold on her, and with his brute strength, used her body to fuck himself with.

Grinding her pussy onto him, she didn't fight him because she wanted him just as much. Holding onto his shoulders, she took over, thrusting onto his cock. She watched his cock fill her, and wished she could see it better, but there was no way for her to see it better unless they did it with mirrors surrounding them.

He held her tightly as he fucked her, going deep within her.

She screamed his name as his cock pounded inside her. Jacob grabbed the back of her head, pulling her toward him so that he took possession of her mouth. He swallowed all of her kisses, and held her tightly as she screamed his name, wanting more, needing more.

"That's it, baby. Come all over my cock. Fuck my cock. Use me, Lou."

Lou rode him hard, taking what she wanted, and he did the same, using her body for his own pleasure. She loved every second of it. Jacob consumed her, set her on fire, and held her tightly as he did so.

"Yes, yes, yes," she said.

"Fuck, baby, I'm going to come. Touch yourself, bring yourself off."

She reached between them, and started to finger her clit. Her orgasm was so close that all it took was a few flicks of her clit, and she came, squeezing his dick.

Jacob growled as he erupted within her, filling her with his cum. She collapsed over him, resting her head on his shoulder, as they both panted, trying to catch their breath.

"I'll be moving you in tomorrow. Me, my brothers, and Riley."

"My parents are going to try and worm themselves into your life."

"I don't give a fuck. I want you, not your parents. Are you going to let them dictate the rest of your life?" he asked.

She sighed, lifting her head to look him in the eye. "You really don't care?"

"I care, but I only care about you. Not them. I can handle them, Lou. Trust me."

"They suck everything dry, and they will use our relationship to better themselves. I don't want your parents to hate me." She liked Maddox and Charlotte

Denton. They were wonderful parents.

Jacob sighed. "You're going to have to trust me. My parents are not going to judge you based on what your parents think. Besides, I've already organized it so they're here to move your stuff here. You've got no choice."

"Oh my God, your ego knows no bounds."

"Not when I'm going after what I want, and I want you." He tugged her toward him, claiming her lips.

She felt his cock swell within her, and she gasped. "Again?"

"What can I say? I've got over three months to make up for."

Chapter Eleven

"Seriously, you couldn't find a company you trust to move this stuff?" Landon asked, lifting one of the futon chairs.

"Why would I do that when I've got five strapping brothers ready and waiting for me to use them?" Jacob opened the door. "Be careful with that," he said.

"Stop being mean," Lou said, moving past him. She tried to help Landon, but he caught her around the waist.

"Remember this is the man who beat your brother's face to a bloody pulp." Jacob spoke loud enough for Landon to hear.

Lou tensed. "You're right. You can certainly handle the chair by yourself." She folded her arms over her chest, and Jacob smirked at his brother.

"That's not very nice," Riley said, coming into the room carrying two boxes from her kitchen. "That was all in the name of sport, and you're using it to stop her working hard."

"See, Riley doesn't hold a grudge. We're totally friends, right, Riley?" Landon asked.

"Total BFFs all the way." Riley clapped Landon on the back. "I'm still not helping you carry that chair. I've heard you've spent most of your down time playing games. You're not going to catch any girls by becoming a couch potato."

Lou laughed and moved away from him. Jacob caught her by the waist, tugging her against him. "You see, I told you that my brothers would be more than happy to help."

"We didn't have a choice. On pain of death, you better be there, I think those were the words," Gideon said, entering the apartment.

"You're all making my apartment look small," Lou said.

"You don't have a lot of stuff," Charlotte said, coming out of the kitchen with a box of her own. Maddox was following close behind her with two more boxes.

"I thought I'd gotten a lot."

"In your new place, it's going to make everything seem so small. Jacob will take you out shopping." Charlotte winked at her and moved out of the apartment.

"I'm going to pack up the bedroom." Lou patted his hands, but Jacob wouldn't let her go without taking the kiss he wanted. He saw she looked sad, so he followed her.

"What's up?" he asked.

She had opened a wardrobe and started taking out some of her clothes. "Nothing, why?"

"You're just a little quiet." He moved past her, going to her clothes, and taking a bunch out. She was removing the hangers and folding them up, so he did the same.

"It's nothing."

"Lou, babe, you're going to have to trust me."

She sighed, dropping the folded dress on the bed before turning to him. "Are you really ready for this? Moving in is a huge step."

He chuckled. "You think I don't know that?"

"I'm trying to be serious."

"Lou, you're always serious, and it's time that you stop being serious, and start having some fun." He placed the skirt that he'd been folding on the bed and caught her hips, pulling her against him. His cock nestled against her stomach, and if it wasn't for all of his family, he'd have taken her again. They hadn't gotten a lot of sleep last night as he hadn't been joking in the bath. Three months was a long time to go without, and he'd done his best to make up for the lost time. "If I could have, the first night I saw you, I'd have gotten you to move in."

"You're not being serious," she said.

"I'm being totally serious. I think it's time I tell you about the Denton men." He stared into her eyes.

"Is this something about the Denton legacy?"

"It is, and it's so much more. Tell me what you know?"

"The work you do, the jobs you have to take. It's all part of the family legacy. You're born into it," she said.

"That's part of it. The other part, well, let's just say I didn't believe it until I met you."

"I'm confused."

Cupping her cheek, he stroked his thumb across her lip. "It happened to my father, my uncles, my grandparents, to all of the male family line. We've not had a lot of women in our family. Tamsin is the first girl in three generations at least."

"Okay, so if we ever had kids, they'd be all boys? Is that what you're trying to say to me."

He shook his head. "The moment we see the woman destined to be ours, we know."

Lou frowned. "Destined?"

"I know, it makes me sound completely crazy but the men in our line, we're fated to love one woman, to be so consumed by her."

"You're starting to sound crazy." She placed her hand to his forehead. "Are you okay? Maybe you're sick."

"It's true, Lou," he said.

"It is," Maddox said, coming into the room,

followed by Charlotte. Jacob turned toward his parents.

He held Lou in his arms, thankful she didn't try to escape him.

"No one can feel like that."

Maddox shrugged. "It's the way of the Dentons, honey. We see the woman who is supposed to be ours, and the rest is history. We don't have a choice, and we fall in love."

She looked at Jacob. "You knew?"

"The moment I saw you at the after party of the fight with Landon and Riley."

"On the stairs?"

"No, before that. You had your back to me, and I just needed to talk to you, to be around you."

"You've got no choice?" she asked. "That is horrible. You can't love me."

He grabbed her face with both hands, resting his head against hers. "Don't, Lou. I love you, and it has only gotten stronger."

"We women don't feel it straight away," Charlotte said. "They have to work to make us fall for them, Lou."

She didn't pull away from him. "This is what you've been doing," she said. "Making me fall for you."

"I want to spend the rest of my life with you." He took hold of her hand and placed it over his heart. "I wish you could feel what's in here every time I look at you."

"But you're not given a choice."

"It's not like that. We want you, but it's not like we'll rape you to get what we want, Lou. I saw you, and I just knew you were supposed to be mine. I wanted to make you happy, to give you everything you need." Jacob kissed her lips. "Trust me. This is what I want. I love spending time with you. You're in here, Lou, and there's no getting away."

"Even if I wanted to, I couldn't walk away, Jacob. How could I not fall in love with the guy who tried to sweet talk my landlord so he could get me a puppy?"

Jacob's cheeks heated. "I've got a surprise for you when we get home," he said.

"What?"

"You'll see it when we get there. You're not angry at me?" he asked.

Lou chuckled. "Jacob Denton, you're a tough guy who can hold his own in a fight, and yet you're asking me if I'm angry at you."

"I don't love any of those men, Lou. I only love you. I'd die protecting you."

She shook her head.

"We're going to make ourselves scarce," Maddox said.

They both turned in time to see his parents walking out of the room.

"I know I'm not the best guy—"

"Shut up. I've lived my whole life with my parents telling me I should and shouldn't do. That's is not what this is about. I love you, Jacob, and even though I'm a little shocked by your revelation, I can handle it." She pressed a kiss to his lips. "I'm still going to be working for Frank."

"No."

She silenced him once again with a finger to his lips. "You don't get a say, mister. I'm not going to be sitting at home waiting for you. I've got to do something, and even though being a waitress isn't supposed to be all that thrilling, I like it. I like Frank. He's a sweet man."

Jacob shook his head this time. "I don't have a say right now?"

"Nope, you don't. I don't want there to be secrets

between us."

"There won't be."

"I also believe in being faithful."

"Lou, I've not even looked at another woman since I saw you."

He cupped her face, tilting her head back, and claiming her lips. "I love you."

"I'll never get tired of hearing that." She kissed him back, and Jacob finally knew why his father constantly loved going home. There was something about being with the woman you love that just made everything right.

****

Later that night, Lou straddled Jacob's waist, kissing him deeply. Her apartment was completely empty, and all of her stuff was packed in boxes in his garage, ready for when she wanted to unpack, which she'd do soon. Right now, she was kissing the man she loved. Who knew that Jacob Denton had a sensitive side?

Her gift had been a St. Bernard puppy.

She had fallen in love instantly.

"If I knew getting you a puppy would get me this, I'd have gotten one for you months ago."

Lou leaned back, pulling her shirt over her head so that she was completely naked. His bed was huge, and they were in the center. Jacob also made sure that he had mirrors at convenient places around his room. There was one above his bed, and on either side, at the base, and then on the wall on the end of his bed. He liked to watch.

The first time she saw his room yesterday, she'd been rather shy, not wanting to see herself from everywhere. She saw past herself, to them, and that was where she'd come to love his mirrors.

Jacob ran his hands up her chest, cupping her tits.

"Fuck, baby, you know how to make a guy feel

thanked." He pinched her nipples, and she moaned as he rubbed the hardened peaks.

She really couldn't believe this was happening.

He glided his hands down to spread the lips of her pussy. Lou gasped as he fingered over her slit, stroking her clit. He circled her hard bud before dipping down to sink inside her pussy.

"This is mine now," he said.

"Yes." She didn't want any other man. Jacob had invaded every single one of his senses.

He pumped inside her, and she stared down, watching his fingers slide inside her with ease. Tonight wasn't about her, so she batted his hand away, and moved to the point that she was kneeling in front of him. Taking hold of his rock hard cock, she pumped the length from base up to the top. Flicking her tongue over the tip she tasted his pre-cum. Taking the entire head into her mouth, she sucked him in deep.

Jacob hissed, wrapping his fingers into her hair and holding tightly. She sucked him until he went deep into her mouth. She pulled away and started to bob her head, taking more of him inside.

Glancing up, she saw his gaze was trained on her. She flicked her tongue over the tip, and he groaned.

"Babe, you're teasing me on purpose. I'm not going to last." He released a groan, and she hummed, taking more of him into her mouth. He tasted musky, and his pre-cum leaked onto her tongue. She swallowed him down, wanting to give him the kind of mind-numbing pleasure that he'd given her.

Tightening her mouth around him, she cupped his balls, teasing them.

"Fuck, babe, I'm going to come."

She didn't stop, working his dick as the first of his cum spilt into her mouth. Lou swallowed him down, and she moaned as the salty taste of him slid down her throat.

"Fuck, baby."

When she pulled away, Jacob flipped her over, kissing her neck, and then moving down to her tits. He sucked on each nipple in turn, and then glided down, his tongue creating a trail down her body.

He spread her legs open, spreading the lips of her pussy, and sliding his tongue between her folds. She cried out as he caressed her clit, sliding down to plunging inside her cunt.

"I could spend the whole night tasting your sweet pussy." He sucked her clit into his mouth, and she whimpered unable to contain her pleasure.

"Yes, yes, yes," she said, begging him.

He fucked her with two of his fingers, going deep within her as he tongued her clit. Lou came within seconds of his tongue teasing her over and over again. Jacob further shocked her as he slid deep, his cock already hard. "I can't get enough of you." Gripping her hips, he started to work in and out of her, taking his time as her pussy tightened around him.

She thrust up to meet him, and when that wasn't enough, he pulled out of her, flipping her onto her knees, and sliding in deep. He wrapped his fingers in her hair, and lifted her head up. "Look at us, Lou. Watch as I fuck you, and know there's not going to be any other woman. You're the woman who owns my heart, and I will do everything in my power to keep you happy, and never let you go."

He kissed her neck, and she gave herself over to him completely. She didn't want to fight her feelings for him anymore.

They came together, holding each other tightly, and Lou would do anything to keep them in their happy bubble.

Chapter Twelve

Two months later

Jacob looked around at the people at the underground fighting ring, and he couldn't shift the uneasiness that had settled deep in his gut. It had been two months since Lou had moved in with him, and he was going to ask her to marry him later tonight. However, his parents had asked him to see the Moores as they were constantly badgering Landon, trying to get him to fight. He saw Abel, Gideon, and even Damian had come along with him. No one fucked with a Denton, and they didn't like how Landon was being approached, even at high school.

Riley was around the back going to get his parents, and he'd taken Lou with him as he did have every intention of taking her out to dinner in order to ask her to marry him. Of course that hadn't happened. His father had called, asking for him to come to this fight, and to let the Moores know to stay away from Landon.

"I don't like this," Jacob said, looking around at the overcrowded basement of a nightclub. The Moores were the ones who organized the fight, and this one looked like it was going to get ugly. He saw the violence simmering in every single person. They were all out for blood, and with blood, there was money.

"Something is going down tonight," Abel said. "I suggest we get our warning out to Moores, and then leave. I don't want to be around when the shit hits the fan."

Jacob agreed and squeezed Lou's hand.

"Do you want me to stay here?" she asked.

"You've got no chance. I'm not leaving you in this shithole. Stay beside me, do not let go of my hand."

He shouldn't have brought her with him.

Men and women shoved him hard, and he was gritting his teeth as he tried to protect his woman. He saw Riley coming out of the main changing areas with his parents behind him. Everything seemed to slow down as the noise dimmed. Jacob watched a man approach the main changing area, going into his jacket. Even from the short distance, he saw the rage. The gun was drawn, aimed, and before Riley could do anything, the man shot three times. Jacob let go of Lou as everyone started to scream running for the exits. He grabbed his gun, aimed, and fired. The man got hit and went down. His brothers and the Moores were the only people within the basement as most were clamoring to get out of the exits.

"No, no, no, no, no," Lou said, rushing toward Riley.

Jacob kept his gun trained on the man on the floor, bleeding out, and Abel took over.

Blood pooled on Riley's shirt, and Lou pressed down on each patch of blood. Tears spilled down her cheeks.

"You hold in there, Riley. Don't leave me okay?"

"That's … going … to … be … diffi … difficult."

"Call an ambulance," Lou said, not taking her eyes off her brother. Jacob was already dialing.

He gave them the location, not caring if this would put the Moores in a difficult position.

"Who is he?" Lou asked, pointing at the man on the floor.

"He lost a fight," her mother said.

"What? He lost a fight? What happened to security?" Jacob asked. "Tonight, there was overcrowding in this fucking place. What happened to the security keeping an eye on people who enter?"

One promise was all Loud had asked, and right now, he'd broken that damn promise.

"It was fucking greed," Lou said. "Wasn't it? You just couldn't handle turning money away."

"Lou…" Riley said, coughing.

He was getting paler, and the blood beneath him was pooling out. Jacob stared into his eyes, and knew there was no way he was going to be able to save him.

"Take … care … of … her."

"Riley, shut up. Don't say things like that," Lou said.

"Listen … to him … Lou. Don't … be a … bitch."

"Stop it, Riley. Please stop."

"It's his … time … to take … care of you." Riley did his best to smile. "Love you." He stroked her cheek, and Jacob saw the brotherly affection there. A second later, his hand fell. He took a breath, and all was silent.

"Riley? No, no, no, Riley."

The doors opened, and Jacob grabbed Lou, pulling her off the body and holding her.

Riley was dead, and he wasn't coming back.

****

Later that night, Lou sat in the waiting area at the hospital with her knees drawn up against her body. She was tired, but she felt nothing. Part of her was empty inside, and when she stared down at her hands, she saw his blood, her twin's. Abel and Gideon were watching her, and Jacob was taking care of everything. She felt nothing other than relief that she still had him. He was the only rock in her life, the man she loved.

But Riley was dead.

Dead.

Her throat was thick, and she rested her head against her knee.

"Oh, honey," Charlotte said, coming to kneel in front of her.

She couldn't even bring a smile.

"Hello."

"Has she seen a doctor?" Charlotte asked.

Abel shook his head. "There's no need for her to. This is how to—"

"To deal with losing a loved one," Lou said.

"Would you like to stay with us tonight?" Charlotte asked.

"What happened to my parents?" she asked.

"They've been taken into custody," Maddox Denton said. "Would you like us to see about getting them released?"

She shook her head. Her parents were the reason Riley was dead. Lou couldn't order their deaths. She wouldn't want that on her own conscience, let alone that of her man. She shook her head. "I want you to make sure they can never get out."

Jacob entered the room. She felt him, and looked up to see the concern in his eyes, and the guilt. No, she didn't want his guilt. This was not his fault. She needed his love, and to know that everything was going to be okay with his arms wrapped around her.

"Everything is done."

"You don't want your parents to get out?" Charlotte asked.

"I want them to rot in prison for the rest of their lives." She got to her feet, and Charlotte stood. "Thank you for your concern, but I'm going to go home to bed." She moved toward Jacob, taking hold of his hand. Her rock. He squeezed her. "Thank you all."

Lou didn't remember the drive home, nor did she recall the shower, and how she got to sitting on the end of the bed with a brush in her hand. Jacob came into the room, kneeling in front of her.

"I'm so sorry, baby, I broke my fucking promise." He placed his head in her lap, and she stared at his bent head, frowning.

"What?" She stared into his eyes as he lifted up. "I don't know what you're talking about. You've got nothing to be sorry about."

"I made you a promise to keep Riley safe. It was the only thing you asked of me, baby. That's all you wanted, Riley to be safe."

"You think he died because of you?"

"I saw him pick up the gun. I couldn't get mine fast enough."

She shook her head, cupping his face. Lou saw the guilt, but she didn't want him to feel it. "No, this has nothing to do with you. Do you hear? Nothing. Do not blame yourself for what happened tonight. Mom and Dad are the reason Riley's dead. Their greed to constantly have more people betting. They didn't even use security, and they should have. This has nothing to do with you, and everything to do with them. They're the ones at fault, not you." She stroked his cheeks. "I'm in pain, Jacob. It hurts." She pressed a hand to her chest. "I feel like I've been torn in two, and there's no going back from it. Please, help me make it better."

He lifted up, kissing her lips and settling her in bed. Jacob climbed in behind her, holding her tightly as she sobbed for her brother. Throughout it all, Jacob held her, and for that, she was thankful.

Chapter Thirteen

The whole of the Denton family were with Lou at Riley's funeral. They made sure to see him off properly. Jacob held onto his woman, giving her as much support as he could. Her sorrow cut him deeply. There was nothing he could do, and those days before and after the funeral were the hardest. Lou didn't go to work. She didn't do anything other than sob, screaming, and crying. Jacob didn't go into work either. He asked his father to give him the time needed to support his woman.

His entire family took their turn visiting and taking care of Lou. A couple of weeks afterward, Lou woke up, and she decided to go to work. Her grief was still there, but Jacob got Oliver to follow her at a safe distance. He made sure she was looked after, never letting her go anywhere without a guard of some kind.

The days passed turning into weeks, and those weeks turned into months. The pain lessened, and after a time, she started to smile again. They would go every Sunday to Riley's grave, and when her parents were sentenced she seemed to be at some peace. Their lawyer had mounted a case against the Moores, and they had even gone out to find others who had suffered at their hands.

The Denton reputation was intact, and they even earned more respect for seeing justice dealt. Jacob, himself, had been disgusted to hear of some of what happened at the Moores' hands. They took men and women off the street, and pitched them against some of the toughest fighters. It wasn't a fair fight, and they would be dumped in a field somewhere. The Dentons were monsters, but they had a set of morals which they lived by. They didn't set out to kill innocents, and especially not dragging people off the streets.

"When are you going to ask her?" his father asked.

It was a Sunday, and they were at his parents' for dinner.

"Today." His brothers were in another room, and his mother was with Lou.

"You don't think it's too soon?"

"I love her, Dad. If she's not ready, then I'll have no choice but to accept that."

He held the ring in his palm and closed his hands around it. Jacob had been going to ask her on the night that her brother was killed.

"She's got us, Jacob. She's in love with you. I don't see a reason for her to turn you down." Maddox slapped him on the back.

Leaving the room, he made his way toward the kitchen.

Lou was peeling chicken as his mother beat some mashed potatoes. She had lost a little weight, which grieved him. He loved her so much, and even though he had broken his promise, she wouldn't let him blame himself. Riley, as far as Jacob was concerned, had died on his watch, and there was no way he'd be able to take that back.

Leaning against the doorframe, he held onto the ring in his pocket, and stared at her.

Why are you waiting?

Stepping into the kitchen, he moved behind her, and kissed the back of her neck.

"What's up?" she asked, finally smiling when she saw him. He loved her smile.

"Nothing. I just wanted to make sure you were okay."

"I'm doing good." She turned around, wrapping her arms around his neck. "You don't have to worry. I'm here, and I'm alive. Riley, he told me to give you a chance, and he'd been telling me long before he passed."

"I should have been there."

"Jacob, you were there." She visibly swallowed. "Riley wouldn't have been able to say goodbye if you hadn't been there. I know he enjoyed working with you, and he considered you a brother he never had." She cupped his cheeks. "Please, stop carrying this guilt. I've told you all the time, I don't blame you. Riley's death, it's not your fault. Don't think it is." She snorted. "You should know by now that if I thought for a second it was your fault, I'd be a bitch." She laughed, and Jacob saw the woman he'd fallen in love with, making a little joke.

"I love you," he said, wrapping his arms around her.

"I love you, too. So much."
****

Lou had never thought for a second that she would be angry at Jacob. Being in the hospital even after Riley had been pronounced dead, she's been so relieved that she hadn't lost Jacob as well. Riley had been taken to the morgue, and she'd sat in the waiting room, wishing that it had all been a horrible dream. It hadn't been. Still, all the time, she'd been thankful that Jacob hadn't been hurt.

She loved Jacob, and she never wanted to be without him. It would kill her, and she'd rather die than live without him. What had happened at that fight had been at the hands of someone who Jacob had no control over. The man had been aiming at her parents, and Riley had got in the way.

Kissing Jacob's lips, she smiled. She had a family, and in her heart, she knew that Riley would be more than happy with that.

"I love you, Jacob. You've not broken any

promises to me."

"Good, because I'm now about to keep a promise that I made to Riley." He went down on one knee, and she was frozen.

"You don't have to do that." She touched his hand with the intention of pulling him to his feet, but he wouldn't let her.

"This is not just about what Riley would want. This is what I want." He was down on one knee, and staring up at her. She saw the love in his eyes, and when she glanced around the room, she licked her suddenly dry lips. All of his brothers, his parents were watching them. "Lou, I love you. I can't give you fancy words, but I can give you me. No one else will ever love you the way that I do. Your brother wanted you to be with someone you really wanted, and I know that man is me. Louisa Moore, will you marry me?"

Tears filled her eyes and spilled down her cheeks. She stared at the simple diamond ring, and she nodded. All of her life she had tried to defy her parents, promising she'd never marry, but this man, this wasn't about defying her parents.

"Is that a yes?"

She nodded.

"I'm going to need you to speak up, babe."

"Yes, it's a yes. I love you, and I want to be your wife."

He got to his feet and wrapped his arms around her, lifting her off her feet. The moment he put her down, each of his brothers took their turn to hug her. Tamsin wrapped her arms around her waist, and she held onto her. This was her family now.

Later that night after Jacob had made love to her, she stroked his arms, staring up at the ceiling.

"Talk to me, babe," he said.

"It's nothing."

"We don't have to get married straight away."

"I don't mind about the wedding or anything like that." She rolled over so that she was facing him. "What if you wake up one day, and wish you'd married someone else?"

"That's not going to happen, Lou. I told you, I love for a lifetime, and I know I love you." He reached out to stroke her check. "You've got me for the rest of your life, and that is never going to change."

She closed her eyes, resting her head against his. "I love you."

"Love you too, babe."

He tilted her head back and took possession of her lips.

"Surreal." It was the only way to describe what had happened to her life within the past year. She'd become part of Jacob's life, lost her brother, and found her soul mate. When she thought of Jacob that was what she thought of him. He was her soul mate.

Jacob chuckled. "Our life has only just started. We've got the rest of our lives to make it even more surreal."

Lou couldn't wait, and she looked forward to the years to come.

Epilogue

One year later

"Are you okay?" Frank asked.

Lou turned toward her boss and smiled. "Yes, I'm fine."

She waited for Ben to finish her order as she stared at the clock. It was her birthday, and Jacob hadn't even been there when she woke up.

Of course, Jacob had been there for her last birthday. Today had been hard, and she had been scheduled to work. It was hard as all she had to remember was the birthday of her twin brother. She still missed Riley, and there were times that she forgot he was gone. Jacob and the whole of the Denton family had helped her deal with the loss. Jacob had helped her during the worst part of her life. Lou hated the way she had been to Jacob in the beginning, being a huge bitch to him. She was an idiot, and every time she thought back to their first encounter, she cringed at her own behavior.

"Here you go, honey," Ben said, handing her the drinks.

"Thanks."

She walked the tray toward the table of men who were regulars. The club was packed with customers today, and they were keeping her busy.

Pam, who was giving a performance, walked off the stage, and the lights went off, plunging the room into darkness. Lou paused and stayed still so she didn't bang into anyone.

The sound of a microphone being tapped drew her attention back to the stage.

"Forgive me for interrupting your night, but today is my girl's birthday. I wanted to do something special, but I know today is a great day, as well as painful for her. So, I'm going to do my best." The lights came on, and Jacob was on stage with all of his brothers beside him, and they all started to sing happy birthday to her.

Jacob climbed off the stage and weaved his way toward her.

She circled the ring on her finger, showing the world that she belonged to a man, this man. Jacob Denton, the man coming toward her.

He placed the mic on the nearest table and wrapped his arms around her. She loved it when he did that.

"Happy Birthday, baby," he said.

"Thank you."

"Today you should be surrounded by your family, and that is us."

"I'm sorry I had to work."

"I know, but you don't have to work alone. I'd already planned this with Frank for your birthday. You and I both know you needed to work today, to help you through. I made sure Frank put you to work," Jacob said.

This man, he knew her better than she knew herself. He took hold of her hand and walked her toward the bar. She followed Riley's advice, and she had stopped being a bitch. Jacob was not going to leave her, and there was no one to fight. "I'll have two whiskeys," he said.

She went to sit down, and Jacob stopped her, placing her on his knee.

"To Riley, baby." He lifted his drink, and together they saluted her brother. Lou had already been by Riley's grave, and placed some flowers. She and Jacob had done that the day before.

Swallowing the burning liquid, she released a sigh, resting against him. Closing her eyes, she basked in his warmth. It had been over a year since she had lost Riley but she had gained so much.

The Dentons were her family. Jacob, the man she loved, had given her his love, his family, and his trust. Her time with him was the best in the world, and one day soon she'd be ready to start a family.

"Are you okay?" he asked, kissing her neck.

"I'm more than good. I've got you, and I know that Riley would have been happy."

He rested his hand against her stomach. "I think it's time for us to start our family, Lou."

"You're ready for that?"

"We've been together long enough. You're the love of my life, Lou. It's not going to disappear. It's only going to get stronger." He kissed her lips, and she closed her eyes. Around them, the noise picked up as another woman walked on stage, but to Lou, she was only interested in her husband, the man who owned her heart and soul.

The Denton family legacy was known to many as a rumor. They were men with vicious reputations, known for being lethal in conducting business. They were a crime family, and feared around most states, but when it came to their women, they fell hard. Staring into Jacob's eyes, Lou saw his love, she saw his desire, and she loved every part of him.

She didn't fall in love with him instantly. Over time she'd fallen in love with him, and that was the best part of all.

No matter what happened between them, they would survive together, and she couldn't wait to see what the future held for them. Lou looked out toward the stage where his brothers were gathered around, hollering at the woman. She looked forward to watching each of them fall, one by one.

"Are you ready to go home, and I'll give you a real birthday present?" Jacob asked.

Lou followed him.

Nine months later, Riley Denton came into the world, screaming.

The End

EVERNIGHT PUBLISHING ®

www.evernightpublishing.com